life and time of professor ennui pidawee

LIFE AND TIMES OF PROFESSOR ENNUI PIDAWEE

Tom Weathers

mount holly
possumgolightly press

ISBN 978–0–578–00523–2

Published by Possumgolightly Press

Mount Holly, NC USA

possumgolightly.com

Covert art, "Flower Buzzard", by Allie Michal Costner and Paw Paw Krackoo.

Dedication

To Leigh who said I ought to do it, to the readers of early versions who said they liked it, and to the conveniently dead whose silent acquiescence made it easier (but whose voices made it necessary).

What it is

A short memoir in three parts.

HISTORY is about the author and some characters he has known (a transvestite, an entrepreneur, a rocket scientist, a beatnik, a martial artist, a movie star, and a fool, to name a few). These stories, taking place from 1945 to 1961, are generally true.

PRE-HISTORY is about the author's parents and grandparents. Occurring before 1945, these stories are generally not true, or are at least imagined. It is through these tales that the author tries to figure out what made his folks the way they were (and explain how he got to be such a pidawee).

DEATH is about the passing of the author's mother in 1955 in Shelby, North Carolina (at the Center of the Known Universe – where all explanations come together).

Although not explicitly about the South, it is a Southern Book. It's got crazy white people, Magical Negroes, muscadine grapes, livermush, dynamite, undertones of violence, and guns - lots of guns.

Regarding pidawees

The book is also about pidawees, at least symbolically.

"Pidawee" was the author's mother's euphemism for the male private member, as in, "little boys have little pidawees, heh heh". Mid-way through the project, he adopted the name as a way to distract from the grandiosity of a memoir about nothing memorable. He would wrap his self-aggrandizement with self-abnegation. He now understands there is more to the title. The cover up is part of him, part of the book - mixed in with all the death and stuff.

He understands that although his father told him to go forth and be a big deal, his mother whispered, "pidawee, pidawee, pidawee" – and that therein lies his tale.

Regarding order

As with any book, this book's order comes from the top and the bottom. The division of related chapters into three parts provides the top-level order. The author's own psyche, emerging from underlying personal and family muck, defines the bottom.

Contents

HISTORY

1945 – 1961

Baltimore

Shelby

Troy

West Palm Beach

Baltimore

In was 1945, a big year…

I experienced true love, either for Genie, the pretty little girl who lived behind us, or for her big friendly white dog.

Franklin Roosevelt died. Picking up on the reaction of the adults around me, I was filled with nameless dread.

I had my best fight ever. The other boy might have been bigger but I was not afraid. I felt like somebody else. It took place in the vine-covered lot behind our house, in a clearing that was like a green cave, or a womb, or a tomb. Children from the neighborhood gathered in a circle around us. They didn't say anything, just shuffled their feet in the moldering leaves, waiting. In my mind's eye I see the punch delivered and the boy going down. I feel the impact traveling like adrenaline up my arm, into my soul.

Little Boy and Fat Man immolated themselves in mushroom clouds over Hiroshima and Nagasaki and I ran around and around the little gray clapboard house where we lived in a wartime development of similar houses. I don't remember now why I ran, but I do recall that I felt as light as a feather, that I could have gone on forever. It was the best running I did until Junior Senior night 12 years later in the jungle near Jupiter Beach when I was chased by a band of marauding lower classmen and managed to escape by jumping a 10-foot drainage canal.

I went with my father and a man in his car to a gun store on the outskirts of Baltimore. Pistols were displayed on one side of the store, long guns on the other side. A gray wooden model of a water cooled machine gun hung from a wall near the door. It was dark inside. Another man took a small revolver from a glittering glass case and let me hold it. The pistol fit my hand perfectly.

I dreamed of bloody bodies and woke up screaming, turned around in the bed, unable to move, caught in the sheets like a bug in a spider's web.

I was followed by my sister into my parent's bedroom. She was about 16 months old, a toddler. She was probably always behind me. I slammed the door on her finger. I said no I didn't mean to do it, but my mother screamed and beat me anyway. Her mouth was a black pit.

A policeman came to the back door and I lay spread eagle on the kitchen floor, pretending to be dead, filled either with fear or guilt (the distinction is no longer clear). My mother was embarrassed and the policeman laughed.

Fifty five years later there were the dreams that I jotted down the next morning as crude little poems...

My companion

the ever unseen

and I

crawled under a house

exposing a shallow grave

from which proclaimed

a small outstretched hand.

It was not our doing

but we still were filled with shame and dread

worried that we too had secrets

waiting to be uncovered.

We visited a college where I wandered for a while

with an older woman

telling her how it was

when I was here

and how much had changed

not getting across

the extent of my confusion.
Then, I asked a scientist where the classrooms were.
As if expecting our arrival
he took us in his large old car
across the school
through a gate
into a field of industrial achievements
poised, artfully,
like spacecraft
or oil wells
arriving finally at a house,
reminding me of 1945.
We walked to the back,
where
in a dining room
also reminiscent of that era
the scientist held a blood-red
retarded baby
and warned,
"Do not look."
His son ,
the baby's father said,
"It's not so bad."
and left.
I thought so too
until I saw the baby boy's misshapen mouth.
Evidently angry at his affliction
the scientist shook the boy a little
and said, "We must not tell."
In clear language

the child replied,

"We must not tell."

In August the war ended; my father was laid off from Martin Aircraft, and we moved back to Shelby, North Carolina (to the Center of the Known Universe).

Hard Babies

At the Center of the Known Universe...

It was 1946.

We lived on Lee Street near the deep woods on the edge of town, in a small white frame house with a white picket fence. It was across the road from Shelby Millwork where my father was the superintendent.

I went to Washington School, not far from Lake Street where we would move nine years later when my mother got cancer. Around the corner from the school, within sight of the playground, was the hospital where she would die.

One morning at recess I rolled my shirt sleeves up over my tiny biceps, imagining that I looked good, like my father or my uncle. The other children were noisy, darting shapes.

Phil materialized from the mob, sneered, and said, "Hey, do you think you are a tough guy?"

I stuttered, trying to come up with a rational answer to his question.

He laughed.

It was 1947.

Don had been teasing me for a year.

We were outside the school about to leave and he said something and I charged him while he waited beneath a small oak tree (that eventually grew big before it was cut down for a parking lot). I threw my body at his knees, trying to knock him down. However, my blow seemed ineffectual and abstract. He laughed while I tossed on the ground.

I was walking home past the big stucco house on Washington Street. Out front was a playhouse with shutters, windows and a Dutch roof. A perfect miniature dwelling. Don said something else and I charged him again. I was losing when Patsy, a classmate, walked by. She grabbed each of us by the back of the neck and rubbed our noses in the soil (that was dark, like chocolate cake). She told us we should behave, laughed, wiped her hands in a grand exaggerated manner, and trotted off in her pretty little dress.

I nearly cut my foot off at Doane's house, jumping from a barrel onto a liquor bottle, slicing the sole my new shoe in half. After that Don became my friend and helped me get around. (Hobbling home, blood pouring from my damaged shoe, I probably would have died if one of the Lutz brothers had not seen me and carried me in his truck to the hospital.)

It was 1950.

I was still at Washington school. The previous year the administrator of the hospital where my mother would die moved to Shelby with his wife, son, and daughter (whose name was Carol). Carol and I, like many other children of the town learned ballroom dancing from the visiting Fletchers. I accompanied Carol to a graduating cotillion in the dining room of the Cleveland Hotel. Eleven years later I would marry her first cousin, Brenda. Their family descended from Jews who became Protestants, although Brenda regretted the part about becoming a Protestant. The Fletcher's daughter became Miss America.

And some say life has no meaning.

I was on the playground with Charles who would grow up to be an attorney and who 57 years later wandered among the crowd at our fiftieth reunion shooting pictures with a really good digital camera. We were near the jungle gym, just outside the cafeteria where they served livermush, cornbread and creamed potatoes. Normally we were friends, visiting one another's homes, trading Hardy Boy books. But today we disagreed about something. Other children heard and closed in. They made us go around the corner where no one could see. They wanted us to fight. They pushed Charles back against the wall. They pushed me in front of him. His head tossed from side to side, hair sticking to the rough brick, hair and tears and snot all over his face, in his eyes

7

and mouth. I didn't hit him. I did not hit them either. My arms had no strength; I was slowed by dreamlike lethargy.

That night I opened the drawer where my uncle kept his pistols, like hard babies, oiled and cleaned, sleeping fitfully on a greasy cloth.

In Front of the Potato House

Dead cat...

Doane and I tried camping in the woods behind my house but it rained and water washed over the trench we had dug around my old army pup tent. At 3:00 AM, we left the tent and wandered around the dark neighborhood like adolescent ghosts.

We walked down Lee Street past Suttle's store where during the day we sometimes got Nehi sodas and Baby Ruth candy bars but which was now empty and gray.

Across the street we sat for a few minutes on the SCO fertilizer bench in front of the potato house where Mr. Suttle stored sweet and Irish potatoes for sale in the winter.

Coming back, gingerly crossing the muddy parking lot, I stepped on a dead cat. It felt soft and squishy under my foot. I jumped and said, "Oh."

Doane laughed and said, "Meow".

Another Place

In the woods...

Doane and I crossed over to another place.

We started beyond the little white frame house at the end of the Lee Street where I lived, entering nearby pine woods where even the smaller children sometimes played

We walked down the trail to the big mossy rock that ran slick with water when it rained. The other children didn't come here often. It was where my uncle tried out newly purchased or traded guns (my favorites were the long-barrel German luger, the big .455 Webley carried by the British in WWI and II, and the 10-gauge shotgun with which I once brought down a small pine tree in two blasts).

Just beyond the rock was the Old Tree, where the trail forked around the base of another hill. The left fork descended toward a spring and the run-down house where Vera our maid lived. I suppose she might have walked up the trail to our house. The right fork snaked behind a colored neighborhood. A limb from the Old Tree angled out ominously over the path and it was easy to imagine that someone had been hung there.

We left the trail and climbed the next hill into deeper, darker woods. No one, not even my uncle or the people from the colored neighborhoods went there.

We pushed past low hanging limbs and spider webs draped in wait for the last insects of Fall. We walked by the cave under fallen rocks that smelled inside of old leaves and animals. Getting lost was not a possibility. The forest was in us as much as we were in it.

Finally we came to the small clear stream known only as The Creek. This was as far as we had ever been. Doane said, "Let's go on."

We forded the stream, crossed a field and climbed the strange cone-shaped hill that had attracted us from the beginning.

Up close the hill seemed steeper and taller. The ground was loose and difficult. Scrub trees grew on the lower slope. The top was covered in patches of broom sage and other dried-up vegetation. Shreds of mica glittered in the low sun. It was windy and the air seemed colder. The sky was a deeper shade of blue.

We looked around. The woods extended in all directions. Except for the field below, there were no signs of people - no houses or roads. It could have been the end of the world, or the beginning.

I said, "This place is spooky."

Doane said, "Let's get back." and we returned to the woods and home.

Magical Negroes

Some magical negroes I have known...

Note: Spike Lee's term, Magical Negro, refers to black characters in fiction (or real life) who exercise magical powers solely for the purpose of developing white people. Think of Will Smith in Bagger Vance. I try to avoid that sort of thing, but the fact that this chapter is here means that I probably haven't. Not really.

The Transvestite Boy

I never knew his name.

I first saw him in 1945 or 1946, when he was about eight, two years older than me. I was sitting with my parents beside our little house on the Lee Street, behind the white picket fence. He must have come from the adjoining black neighborhood where families lived on dirt roads in even smaller houses and observed from sagging porches white women stopping in their cars to pick up or drop off maids, some of whom refused, even when asked, to sit in the front seat. He stood before us, small but righteous, telling about mistreatment by a white person. Perhaps he was returning from Suttle's Grocery down the street where white people bought candy and soft drinks and black people bought most of their groceries. I don't recall my parent's exact response; although, their tone seemed sympathetic. I remember being struck by the unfairness of whatever it was.

My next memory of him is 10 or 15 years later. He was walking down North Morgan Street, wearing tight pink shorts, high heel shoes, and a powder blue blouse tied up over his ribs. He looked neither to the right nor left; his expression was determined, his head up.

After that, I saw him around town for a number of years. He became one of Shelby's minor characters, known as the transvestite boy, or the "morfydike".

(Major town characters included Fred the son of a Greek restaurant family. He screamed, jumped straight up beside people who were about to cross the street, wore a Superman cape and reportedly stabbed his sister. Another was Lenard, the shell-shocked black man who sat in the Dairy Queen, read magazines, made BOOM noises and tolerated the earnest ministrations of white people who, after Wednesday night prayer service, would save his soul.)

The transvestite boy was usually alone. He always looked straight ahead, after a while no longer a boy but not exactly a man or a woman, not proud as he minced down North Morgan Street, but not ashamed either. I don't know for sure what happened to him; I heard that he died.

Aunt Francis

She worked for us when we lived just outside of Shelby in the rental house where my grandfather died 15 years earlier. The house had a horse pasture on one side and a turnip patch on the other. The turnip patch was bordered by a wall of muscadine grapes and when I stood there biting into the leathery fruit, I was reminded of the scene in the Prince of Foxes where Everett Sloan crushed two grapes into juicy pulp, pretending they were Tyrone Power's eyes.

I don't expect Aunt Francis ever saw the Prince of Foxes. She probably never went to a movie. Nor did my grandmother, who stayed with us at the time. Also, I don't expect either woman ever ate grapes and thought about bursting eyeballs.

Aunt Francis lived down a barely passable trail that went beside our house, past the horse barn, past houses scattered like witch huts in the woods and fields, ending eventually at the First Broad River where my great-grandfather Sydney lived in the house that washed away in the flood of 1916. Her house (like his house I imagine) rested on piled up rocks and was sheathed in unpainted pine aged black and gray with orange highlights around the knots. There was no electricity. She walked across the trail to get water from a spring nestled in the side of a hill. My sister and I were invited once into her house. It smelled like cooked pork. Newspapers, fading then, had been pasted on the walls. At the time I thought the papers were for decoration, but they might have been insulation. She kept a hand-painted, unhusked coconut in the corner of the kitchen. It was a memento from her son who had served in WWII. She gave us small cold biscuits, made from buttermilk which she stored in a jug propped on a flat rock in the spring. I don't think this house was her ancestral home, just another place.

My mother, who tended to romanticize people, said Aunt Francis was a saint (e.g., a "magical negro"). Maybe so. But at her house she was just a kindly but tough old woman who gave me a biscuit.

Milton

He drove tractor trailer trucks for Shelby Millwork, where Mr. Daniels was Lord and my father was High Sheriff.

I think that he drove a faded blue Ford truck.

I was allowed to ride with him on some of his trips. Once he pulled the rig on the side of a country road and we walked out in a pasture and split a watermelon that he had picked up along the way. Another time we ate lunch in a black restaurant in Charlotte. It was a bright summer day. We opened a screen door into a cool, dark room with a rich, meat smell. The other patrons were shadowy figures who observed without comment Milton and his pale ward. I had a cheeseburger dripping with chili.

It was my idea to go on these trips. I don't know what Milton thought. I know that he called my father Mr. Tom and did a complex shuck and jive around white people. But he treated me well, which was all I cared about.

Aside: When my mother broke her ankle, Milton's daughter stayed with us and cooked. She was a beautiful reserved girl with café au lait skin and slanting green eyes. Until she came I never knew that bacon did not have to be burned and black, that it could be golden and brown.

Big Jim

Like Huckleberry Finn, my father, and probably a lot of other southern white boys, I knew a "Big Jim".

Jim worked for my father, following, when asked, from Shelby to Troy and back to Shelby. He ended up driving a delivery truck for O.E. Ford, where my father sold building supplies.

Like all the other Big Jims, Jim was kindly (to me anyway) and strong. At Montgomery Millwork, where I helped him operate a glue press, he told me without bragging, that he was certainly the strongest man in the place. He taught me how to use a shovel and if I had asked, would have taught me how to hunt rabbits, not for fun, but for food. He advised me about girls and regarded me as a object of amusement.

I was no more afraid of Jim than I was of death then. However, on weekends he sometimes got drunk and once cut up another man so badly that it took 100 stitches to sew him up. Jim showed me the hawk bill knife that he used, the hooked blade still stained, like a trophy, with traces of the other's blood. Jim said he didn't cut to kill, just to scar. He spent one weekend in jail until my father got him out in time for work on Monday morning.

There was one other black worker at the millwork plant. He was frightened and grinned like a possum. Some of the younger white employees made fun of him. But nobody even looked at Jim.

Skin

We worked together at Palm Beach Millwork, stacking lumber, hauling things. He was a skinny, jittery little man with slick-backed hair, sharp features and light skin. One day, while we sat on a stack of wood, loafing, smoking cigarettes, he told me about the Bucket of Blood, a club in the black part of West Palm Beach. He offered to take me with him one Saturday night, knowing I would not go. He grinned, saying, "Come on white boy. You be a nigger one Saturday night you never be a white boy again."

I always regretted not taking him up on his offer to let me be a nigger for a night.

Stump Man

He was short and broad, like a stump. He sometimes showed up at karate class, near the end, when it was time to spar. He gave the matched gifts of humility and pain, but always in proportion to the recipient's ability to receive.

He waited at the center of the 20 by 30 studio. He wore a black gi, faded gray, cinched by a black belt, also faded. His hair was cropped short, befitting an ex-Marine. His stood with legs spread, arms held down, hands flexed. He resembled Doom. The rest of us (a multi-racial crowd) waited at end of room where Woody (a "kindly" black man) had his old school desk.

When it was my turn, he would look at me, grin like a wolf, and say, "You ready? "

I walked over, feeling the plywood floor flex, peered at his sardonic face, bowed without losing eye contact, then on Woody's command, tapped his old glove with my new glove, stepped back and felt the space around me contract until there was nothing but him and me.

At first, it was just breathing. There was no question of being able to defend myself. But I could learn to breathe while being peppered with stinging kicks and punches. He would hit me, then tell me to relax.

Later I managed to land a few punches and kicks. But he could still get me, one moment there, the next moment here, sliding the blade of his short broad foot under my arm to pummel my ribs. The better I got the harder he hit. And he always told me, "Relax, relax."

Stump Man was pure magic.

Uncle Bob

A pidawee who achieved grace...

Uncle Bob lived with us off and on until my mother died. Then he moved to Phenix City Alabama to be near my Aunt Margaret, his other sister. The last time I saw him in Shelby, he showed me a .45 automatic pistol wrapped in a rag like the baby Jesus and confided that he had recently shot a bothersome youth in the ass, but, that the Phenix City police, whose guns he maintained, agreed it had been necessary.

Others said Bob was troubled; my father said he was a fool. I assumed that I would grow up to be like him.

However, he had his moments.

He once put out a fire. We were living in the old farm house where my grandfather Isaac Yancey was living when he gave up tenant farming and died. The house had electricity but no indoor plumbing and was heated by fireplaces. We got our water from a spigot sticking up from the dirt in the back yard. The fire started in the attic from cracks in the chimney. I remember my father, mother, sister and grandmother dithering in the yard while Bob ran to the spigot, attached a hose, ran back to the house with the hose, climbed up in the attic and put out the fire.

He could shoot. Using a .22 pistol he could hit birds on the wing and snakes at night when everyone got drunk and went out to the creek to gig frogs. Using a pistol, he could also hit rabbits from the back of a bouncing pickup truck when he and the other wild boys chased rabbits from the roads to the fields.

He eventually became a part-time gunsmith. During his early days, when he and I shared a bedroom like older and younger brothers, he fabricated various weapons. He converted a tube-fed Marlin .22 into a full automatic. I remember the sound coming from the woods behind our house, "riip, riip". He also made a muzzle-loading pistol which he fired in the room with the door shut, thinking, I suppose, that my mother wouldn't hear. He was afraid of her. When a sliver of lead from the ill-fitting cylinder of a Harrington and Richardson .22 hit me in the thumb he begged me not to tell her. It stayed there for years. I only told friends, bragging about my wound.

He could blow up things. Not long after World War II (where he had been a 17-year old shell-shocked Marine) he used a lye-based concoction to blow up a utility building next to our house. This was the little white frame house with the picket fence to which we returned after my father was laid off from his war-time job in Baltimore. I was only six years old, but I remember the boom, the red flash, the wood flying, and the people scurrying.

The next explosions occurred nine years later. Bob had returned to the Marines then had been dishonorably discharged because he drove a truck drunk and somebody died. We had moved to the farm nine miles from Shelby on the North Carolina-South Carolina line where my father attempted to be a gentleman farmer. My friend Doane and I discovered a box of dynamite in the tool shed.

Some of it Bob blew up just for fun. He sauntered across the pasture, cigarette dangling from his mouth, tossing sticks of dynamite like bouquets at a wedding.

With some, he attempted to break up large rocks in a field - placing a stick under a rock, lighting the fuse and running. However, most rocks did not shatter but simply flew, intact.

The most productive use for the dynamite was when the well went dry. After trucking sloshing tubs of water from a neighbor, Bob and Jim dug our well deeper. (Jim was the large black man who lived with his family in the little shack on our property and now from this vantage point seems to have also been our property.) It was a hand-dug well just outside the back door. Although not deep, the well was wide, which allowed Bob and Jim to climb down and dig by hand. However, as I recall, the work proceeded slowly so Bob descended by himself and set a charge. He did this several times. He disappeared into the hole and scrambled out a few minutes later. The ground went

WHUMP, and a geyser of mud the color of feces erupted from the cavity in our back yard.

That was the hot dry summer of 1954. Later that summer we moved to Troy then the next year my mother died and, as I indicated, Bob went to Alabama. I understand that he did well there. The few times I saw him, he seemed reserved and almost dignified.

Racing Around Shelby

Driving diversions at the Center of the Known Universe...

Carl and his girl friend picked me up in a nice brown and white, '50 Chevrolet coupe which he let me drive back to Troy, even though I didn't have my license. As I recall, I drove well. My father stayed at the hospital. That was the day in August, 1955 when I became 16 and they did exploratory surgery on my mother at the Baptist Hospital in Winston Salem.

A few weeks later, we returned to Shelby so that my mother could die among old friends. I don't remember how the move was accomplished, if I was asked to pack my socks and jeans and Frye boots and green vee-neck sweater and science fiction books and guns and whatever else I had. One moment we were in Troy where I had found temporary true love with a girl named Leanna who was visiting from Hamilton Ohio, then we were back in Shelby at the Center of the Known Universe.

But I remember the racing.

Sometime I raced with Doane. He drove his father's black 46 Chevrolet coupe. It resembled a hunched-over beetle. I drove my father's 50 Ford. It didn't look like any sort of animal but with the circular member in the center of the grill it did seem to have a surprised, "Oh" expression.

Our racing was mostly in the county along two-lane roads where there were never any police. The cars weren't fast and always seemed about to blow up, but we did manage to squeak the tires when starting off side by side, hunched over big steering wheels, glancing over to see who would go first. And I recall bouncing across a narrow bridge at the bottom of a long hill, dimly aware of the creek and tangled vegetation beneath, seeing the speedometer of the old Ford briefly touch 100 miles per hour.

Often we raced after Young Life. This was a religious organization, sponsored by Baptists I think, that met each week in the homes of students who lived in bigger houses. We sat in warm congenial groups, sang rousing songs, listened to messages, probably had punch and cookies provided by doting parents then when it was over gathered to race around the county before ending up at one drive-in restaurant or another.

It was usually four or five cars. Being fit for racing had no bearing on which cars appeared. One participant regularly showed up in a Willys station wagon. Going around curves, it rocked on its springs like an out-of-control baby carriage. Somebody else raced a Plymouth station wagon. I have a clear image of a boy crawling out the back door window of the station wagon, clamoring across the roof of the tossing car, then crawling in the window on the other side. I don't remember who it was. It might have been Jimmy who grew up to be a building contractor, or Marley who became the architect of a coliseum, but I expect it was Larry who was a writer before he got a mysterious blood disorder and died.

I participated in a few of the races. But more often than not, I rode with Frank to Young Life. Although his blue and white 55 Chevrolet, with its Power Pac, was more fit for racing than most, Frank never raced. He never speeded and always sat erect. That year, he appeared in the Senior Superlative section of the annual as Most Shy Boy. He was peering around a large oak tree, smiling primly at the Most Shy Girl. Both he and the girl had straight hair held in place with generous amounts of oil. 50 years later, after being a realtor, insurance salesman and social worker, he would realize his ambition to drive a bus, then he got lung cancer and died. In one of our last coherent conversations, he laughed and said he was in a "transition period".

The only wreck that I recall was mine.

It happened one Saturday afternoon, not long after we moved. Doane and Larry sat beside me on the Ford's big front seat. It might have been the first time that I had driven by myself with just friends in the car. We were going down a dirt road that was covered in loose gravel. It wasn't far from my Uncle Paul's farm. I was trying, with some success, to make the rear end slide out. Larry said, laughing, "I am too young to die." Then instead of the road, all that appeared through the front windshield was a red clay bank. There was a hollow BAM and the car stopped with the bumper embedded in the bank and the front wheels dangling over the ditch. Uncle Paul pulled us out with his tractor. Although he never talked much, he was sympathetic now. My mother wasn't. When I got back to the little house where we would live for a few months until she went into the hospital for the last time, she told me I should not cause my father this extra trouble. I had the decency to become anxious and throw up.

My mother stopped driving when we came back to Shelby. She never did like to drive and didn't get her license until she was in her thirties and then she nearly killed herself and my little sister on a solo trip back from Alabama. Occasionally I had to drive her. We both hated that. My driving made her nervous and having her fragile and complaining in the front seat made me self-aware.

Christmas At Joe's

My friend the rocket scientist...

Whenever I hear a woman with a sad, sexy voice sing "have yourself a merry little Christmas" I think about sitting in a car parked outside of Joe's house with girls who don't even have faces now.

We were visiting from Florida. It was a year or two before we moved back to Shelby. My sister stayed with one of her friends, maybe Lyn whom I later dated. My father and stepmother stayed with her sister and brother-in-law. I stayed with Joe and his mother. They lived on Lee Street, not far from where we once lived. I first met Joe when he stopped at our house on his way home from Howard Suttle's neighborhood store to tell us that he had lost a tooth but that he would swallow the blood so it wouldn't be wasted. The adults snickered but I thought it seemed practical.

Joe was not like the rest of us. He wore an Army helmet liner to high school because it was cheap and kept the rain off his entire head. He did this even on days when the math teacher was out and Joe taught the class. He enclosed a rocket test stand in an old hot water heater jacket and used the coil from a Model A Ford to ignite soda-straw fuses filled with propellant. After reading an article in Popular Science about the benefits of reclining chairs he built one which he kept on his front porch and in which he encouraged guests to sit and experience the positive affects for themselves.

He made engine noises (going barroom, barroom) when he passed other pedestrians on the street and he barked at dogs from passing cars. Most dogs, hearing him, ran the other way. Possibly some humans also moved aside. Joe had a heavy beard when he was in the sixth grade and though not unnaturally large was unnaturally strong. A previous summer at the City Park pool I saw him lift a would-be bully over his head. (However, he returned the other boy gently to the ground and would never, despite our entreaties, use his strength for retribution.)

I stayed in the bedroom at the back of the house. Joe's room was at the front, near the sidewalk. Model airplanes and rockets hung from the ceiling. In one corner was a model of "Cosmo" the car he someday planned to build. In another corner was a stack of "Nancy" comics. His room had perhaps been intended as a sun porch because the outside walls were all windows. The rest of the house was dark with gray blinds that stayed pulled down all the time. Joe was the light of the house.

I don't remember much about Joe's mother. She had been sick for years and appears and disappears in my mind's eye like a ghost. She didn't talk much to me. Once, when I lied about breaking one of Joe's model airplanes, she called my parents who made me come back and apologize. I don't think she was in the living room that Christmas morning when their family was opening presents and I asked Joe's brother Carl, the price of the pants he had gotten for Joe. Everyone looked at me for a moment, long enough for me to realize what I had done, then Carl smiled and told me. Of course, by then, Joe's mother didn't need to be there because my own shame was adequate.

The house is gone now, torn down in the 1970's to make room for a medical center where they take pictures of radioactive liquids moving through body passages. I had a hiatal hernia photographed at the address where, 20 years before, Joe and I ate breakfasts of peanut butter, butter and mayonnaise on saltine crackers.

Outside of Joe's immediate family, probably few people remember, much less care, about the house. I remember and care because it is part of my dream landscape. It is the dark fading place with peeling wallpaper and cold rooms and kindly, shadowy people.

It is also the place where the night before Christmas, a year or two after my mother died and we moved to Florida to live with strangers, I sat out front in a car snuggled by girls like soft warm blankets.

Bill's Boat

My friend the entrepreneur...

Bill says all we did that summer was watch him build the boat. He sits in the downstairs den of his big house in South Charlotte, where upstairs, in the other den, a 12-foot Old Town canoe hangs artfully on the wall, and describes how he worked while the rest of us witnessed.

He might be right. I don't remember. I'm not even sure of the year. It could have been 1957. That was two years after my mother died and my sister, father and I moved to West Palm Beach where he had a new job. Or, it might have been 1959, when my father brought us back to Shelby because he always came back - from Tijuana, San Diego, Detroit, New York, Rochester, Baltimore, Troy, and now Florida.

I do remember showing up at Bill's house. That would have been the same regardless of the year. We were always showing up at one house or the other, especially if somebody had a project going. Bill was usually good for something; later there would be the Austin Healy, the AJS motorcycle and several other cars. Coleman had an arsenal of new and antique weapons. Joe had a test stand behind his house where he compared the thrust of CO cartridges filled with various home-made rocket fuels, one of which, according to our legends, actually got the interest of the government. I did not have projects yet; although, I did write.

And I remember that it was an ugly boat.

The bow was a big chunk of pine, shaped possibly with a hatchet. The sides and stern were pine planks. The bottom was tongue and groove oak flooring. Several of us helped bend the sides to the bow. I think I remember Bill yelling while Frank and I pushed the planks together. If the screws had come loose, the rebounding lumber could have broken Bill's nose.

Eventually the wood was smoothed, sanded, caulked and painted battleship gray. Over the next several years, I saw the boat in the water twice.

The first time, Coleman, Joe, Larry and I floated down Broad River. It was in the winter, maybe the Christmas when my father visited Shelby long enough to marry my step-mother. Her niece lived with her mortician husband and child over a mortuary where 30 years later my father would be laid out and 15 years after that Frank would be displayed. I spent Christmas Eve in their back bedroom, above the place where they prepared the bodies, wondering if I could smell formaldehyde. The next day, returning home on US 1 in northern Florida, I became so uneasy that I had to ask my father to pull over to the side of the road so that I could throw up.

We put the boat into the river near the big white farm house where Frank's Aunt Charlotte lived. Frank didn't want to ride in the boat; neither did Bill. But Frank hauled the boat to the edge of the river and then picked us up later.

It was a voyage of seven surprises (assigning structure to events that possibly have none).

The first surprise was getting the boat in the water. In movies the frontiersmen seemed to have no trouble launching their birch bark canoes. Bill's oak-bottom boat was another story. It weighed at least 200 pounds. We couldn't carry it down the steep, muddy bank without risking falling into the cold water. We had to push it. Then when the bow slid into the river there was some question as to whether it would come back up or just keep going under like a submerging turtle.

But, the boat floated. That was the second surprise.

The third surprise was the river itself. It seemed more narrow and constrained than seen from my previous vantage points on shore. The mud-splattered winter vegetation grew down the banks in a dense, confused tangle. And the current seemed a lot faster than I had imagined. If the Scotts Irish had such a creation myth, we could have been venturing down a symbolic birth canal, to be reborn at Stice Shoals dam, where Frank waited with a pickup truck to deliver us from the river.

The fourth surprise was the ducks. We carried a couple of Coleman's muzzle loading pistols with which to shoot any ducks that might be sitting on the river. Some ducks did fly back over us, flushed by our noise. The surprise is that we saw any ducks. It wasn't a surprise that we missed them. But it was a surprise, the fifth, that we didn't shoot each other.

The sixth surprise was when Coleman got hung on the overhanging limb. We were floating past a small island in the middle of one of the few wide places in the river. Trees grew down to the edge of the water; the limbs of some projecting outward over the river. We floated under one of them. The person in the front ducked, but Coleman, who was distracted, was scooped out of the boat to hang, belly down, over the limb. I don't remember how we retrieved him I but expect that Joe, who though not abnormally large was abnormally strong, managed to grab the limb and hold the boat still until Coleman could get back in. The surprise was that this was such perfect comedic moment. They don't usually happen in real life.

The final surprise was a bit of elegant dialog, also not common in real life. It was uttered by Larry, who had already started to write and would write more until he died of a mysterious blood disorder 10 years later. He was using a tin can he had retrieved from the river to scoop out water that leaked into the boat. Bent over, resembling a large skinny bird (his nickname was "Beaky") he said, "A bailer's lot is difficult at best."

Finally, just above Stice Shoals dam, Frank helped get us out of the water and we went home. Several years later, I took Mimi, the daughter of the man who operated the dam to the State Theater and watched her move down the aisle, a much more attractive vessel than the one Bill built.

The other episode with Bill's boat was maybe in 1961, not long before most of us married and ceased having these kinds of episodes.

It took place on a small lake on the property of one uncle or another. I don't remember how we got there, I don't remember how the boat got there and I don't remember where the girls came from.

It is just a few images.

An oversize outboard motor has been attached to the boat and somebody, probably Bill, is roaring around the small lake. The bow, the same unlovely chunk of pine, is sticking up at an unnatural angle while the stern throws up a huge wake that is higher than the sides of the boat. Bill, crouched at the back, one hand on the throttle and the other clutching the side of the boat, is actually sitting below the surface of the lake.

The boat is on the bank, resting upside (see the picture at the first of this story). The bottom is beaded, indicating that it was recently in the water. Two girls sit on the boat. One is Sylvia; I don't remember the other one. Bill is also on the boat, lying on his back. He is wearing a tee shirt over bathing trunks and has one knee raised, like a pinup. His expression is coy.

We are standing in a group (the girls are not there so it might have been another time). Johnny is wearing nothing but shorts and a tee shirt, stretched down over his crotch. He seems uncomfortable. I think the boat has sunk.

Then we leave.

20 years later, Bill had another boat, a big classic Kris Kraft, like the one in which Montgomery Clift and Elizabeth Taylor rode in "Place in the Sun". (The rowboat from which Montgomery drowned Shelly Winters was more like Bill's first boat.) Bill toured Lake Wiley in the Kris Kraft with his other "river rat" friends. 10 years after that he acquired a smallish yacht, which he keeps near his weekend house in Charleston. Lately, he has been talking about selling the yacht, saying that he is getting too old to keep it up.

Pidawee cowboy...

It happened in a field on Coleman's father's farm, across the railroad track from Washburn Switch Road. The incident became part of my personal mythology, resulting in an oft-told story combining elements of self-aggrandizement and self-abnegation. The place became the setting for my "on the farm with vaguely disapproving adults" dreams.

I know that Frank and Coleman were there – maybe Doane or Johnny, but not Larry because he was in Miami with his Hitler scrapbook driving a Renault Dauphine flat out all over town, yelling at Volkswagens and Fiats. Joe wasn't there either. He was in West Palm Beach starting his career as a rocket scientist.

It was in the summer of 1961. We were 21 and 22, in the last year of college or, like Joe, in the first year of our first jobs. Next year most of us would be married; in two years about half would be in the Army, and in 10 years one of us would be dead.

We were visiting Coleman because that summer we still lived with our parents and still dropped in on each other without warning, asking, "What do you wanna do?". We went to the field because Coleman had business with men who were working there and we always followed the one with a purpose.

On this day, I was armed with a Ruger single-action .22 revolver. It looked like a cowboy Colt, which was the idea. I wore it in a holster on my side and perhaps sauntered.

Although the others probably did think I was silly, they didn't think I was too silly because they were all capable of the same thing. Coleman had a room full of weapons including antique muskets and a WWI German mortar. Several years earlier, Coleman, Larry, Joe, and I floated down Broad River in Bill's homemade boat, some of us carrying Coleman's muzzle-loading pistols with which we planned to shoot left-over winter ducks. And before that, after I moved to Florida but before Larry moved, they used the same pistols to shoot some sparrows and robins in what became known as the Great Sparrow Bird Hunt. To honor these song bird spirits, my friends spitted the small carcasses over a camp fire that night and ate what was not consumed by the flames.

By 1961 I had pretty much lost any interest in killing animals. The reason I had the pistol was to practice fast draws and impress my friends. Fast-drawing was the craze that year, maybe due to the popularity of TV westerns like Maverick, Paladin and Gunsmoke.

The first draw seemed slow. The bullet kicked up the red clay about 30 feet in front of me. Other than to make sure I didn't hit any of my friends, who as I recall, weren't paying much attention, I didn't aim, just pulled the pistol out of the holster, cocked the hammer and jerked the trigger.

The second draw seemed faster, producing a satisfactory puff of dirt about 20 feet ahead.

The third draw seemed even faster, kicking up soil about 10 feet from my feet. Possibly by this time, the others were paying attention.

The fourth time, I cocked the hammer and pulled the trigger before the pistol cleared the holster. I felt no pain, just sort of a smack. It occurred to me that I hadn't been drawing faster, just pulling the trigger sooner. I didn't look down.

I said to Frank, "Frank, am I shot?"

He made his tee-hee laugh and announced to everybody. "Tom's shot himself in the ass."

Then I looked down. There was no blood, no injury. We speculated that the bullet hit a brad in the holster then ricocheted out the end and away from my foot. I since learned that other, less-lucky fast-draw artists had shot themselves this way.

My friends probably were impressed - after a fashion. I don't know about the adults working in the next field.

Town of Opportunity

Chance to get it right...

Troy, North Carolina is not far from ancient, worn-down mountains, a state park, and several lakes. It is surrounded by farms and forests and is about 30 miles from larger towns.

When we lived there in 1954 and 1955, it had less than 2,000 people. However, because of its relative isolation, the town had acquired more amenities than you might imagine.

There was a downtown hotel. My father and Uncle Bob stayed there in the Spring of 1954, until school was out and the rest of us could follow. They came home every weekend to the farm outside Shelby where my mother, sister and I waited and watched for the dust that billowed up behind the old Ford as it bounced down our red clay road. My father stayed at the hotel again in 1956, this time with me, when we came back for a visit after my mother died. The rooms were not air-conditioned but there was a large ventilation shaft in the middle of the building where the wind moaned late at night. A drug store and a soda shop occupied the bottom floor. They sold paper-back books for 25 cents. I slipped at least one science-fiction novel inside the homemade shirts that my mother sometimes stitched together.

The town also had a movie theater that was opened on Wednesday and Friday nights, and Saturday from midday until midnight. It smelled of urine and rancid popcorn butter, and the floor was sticky with spilled Cokes. When I heard Bill Hailey and the Comets sing Rock Around The Clock in the Blackboard Jungle I knew that I had experienced something momentous.

Next door to the theater was Wimpy's restaurant, the back room being Reese's pool hall where all the smart boys, rich and poor, gathered. The owner lived in the house across the street from us. I tried to impress Bookie, his blonde, 13-year old daughter with my 15-year old prowess and although curious, she was having none of that.

Troy was a town of opportunity.

On the first day of high school both the football coach and the principal greeted me at the front door. They explained, possibly speaking at the same time, splitting my psyche as if this were some sort of tribal rite, that the football team needed players and would I try out. In Shelby I had trouble getting on teams even in gym class so I said yes.

I later learned that Troy had recently switched from five-man to 11-man football and was having trouble getting enough males from the small school to field a team. Although a number of boys showed up at the start of the season, by the last game, after we had lost every contest, there was once again a player shortage. The coach and principal convened a meeting in the auditorium of all the boys. They appealed, as I recall, to school spirit and shame. I got a letter by virtue of the fact that I came to every game. In later years, I also placed well in karate tournaments by competing in classifications where so few showed up that even if I lost all my matches I still got a trophy.

There were other opportunities, not just for me but for all the members of my family.

The town, as I smugly reported back in Shelby, seemed to have an inferiority complex. Anyone from a larger town, even Shelby, was regarded as being more sophisticated – cosmopolitan even. My mother and father, who possibly had never been in such a place, were invited to join the little Montgomery County Country Club. They might have even gone to an event where my mother got to wear the green sequined dress in which she would be buried by Christmas of 1955. She became active in the Methodist church; my father joined the Lions Club and my sister had legions of friends, just as she had in Shelby.

Even I got around, if not exactly anyone's closest friend, then certainly a valued acquaintance of many.

I spent the night at the Tara-size house of the two rich boys, Larry and Charles. They sent the colored caretaker out to get beer from a black bootlegger and we lolled in a bedroom bigger than my house pretending to get drunk. The last time I saw Charles was during my abortive career at NC State, after we came back from Florida when I was trying to become an engineer. I was walking alone down Hillsborough, perhaps just having bought a bottle of wine, when Charles came by in a red Alpha Romeo convertible with a beautiful girl (or maybe two) sitting beside him. He waved grandly and yelled, "I'll see you." If my mother had not gotten sick and we had not left town, I might have ended up working for the two rich boys.

I rode around with the two smart boys, Mike and Lowell. Lowell was wiry and clever. He nearly killed us one night coming back from the drive-in movie. A number of boys were sitting on straight-back chairs in the back of his father's pickup truck. Lowell passed a slower car by driving up an embankment. It wasn't so steep that we fell out, but all the chairs did slide down to the lower side of the truck.

Mike kept a five-foot blacksnake in an activity room located in an outbuilding behind their house and a bottle of a bitter green liquid that he claimed was a drug but which had no affect on me. I never saw him after leaving Troy, but if he made it to Vietnam I could imagine him in the Martin Sheen role as the sensitive soldier who becomes a killer (seeing myself in the same role).

I also spent time, against Lowell's advice, with some of the guys who lived out in Montgomery county. One day, toward the end of the term, I skipped school and ended up in a car with a group going to the park on top of Morrow mountain. Their conversation hinted at real wildness and I was afraid. But Joe, the driver, a fat boy with a solemn baby face, never spoke and handled the car with delicate grace.

There were also girls.

Walking with a church group through town one night, bundled up against the cold, maybe singing Christmas carols, I found myself holding Lorene's hand and regarding how lovely she seemed with her face flushed by the chill. There was Laura at the drive-in movie, in the summer, sitting with me in the back seat of Butch's father's freshly washed Oldsmobile watching a National Geographic film featuring half-naked native girls.

And there was Leanna, the girl who visited from Hamilton Ohio. On her last night in Troy, we walked arm-in-arm around town, ending up on a bench in front of the attractive little hospital where in a few weeks my mother would go in with one problem and come out with another.

Saturday Afternoons

Fading images...

This is an oddly cut movie running in my head.

I see my mother, father, sister and me in the 1950 Ford going to Albemarle or Asheboro. We do this several Saturday afternoons a month. My parents talk; my sister and I retire to opposite corners of the back seat and do not say much.

The stated reason for going is to buy things that aren't available in Troy; although, the only purchase I witness is of my football shoes. When I see the shiny aluminum cleats I wonder what would happen if somebody wearing similar shoes stepped on the back of my hand.

The real reason for going is so that my mother and father can get out of town. They are restless people. In 16 years of marriage they have moved nine times and will move twice again in the next year before my mother dies.

In this interior movie, landscapes become dreamscapes that have been attenuated by time.

On the road to Albemarle my view from the back seat of the old Ford is reduced to uniform stretches of woods and fields, a bridge across a lake bordered in the distance by a dim line of trees, and a restaurant not far from the lake. Sometimes we stop here for lunch. Once after eating a cheeseburger and looking across the water, I experience a connection to something ineffable and grand, but lose it when I have a bowel movement in the toilet, which is paneled in knotty pine and smells of disinfectant.

The view from the road to Asheboro is likewise reduced. On the outskirts of Troy is the Russell family mansion, grand behind an expansive lawn. I once spent the night here. Down the road is the roadhouse where the smart boys and girls gather every Friday and Saturday night. Next comes the town of Biscoe (consisting in my mind's eye of one intersection and one nondescript building). Then there is a left turn, more countryside, and Asheboro.

In my movie, Asheboro becomes just one street. There are no other streets; no connecting roads. One moment we are in Biscoe then we are on this street of store fronts.

We always park at the end of the street, just past the last store, and walk to the other end of the street where the rest of the town disappears. By this time, I am wandering on my own, so while the others do whatever they do I look in store windows. I actually enter one store. They have a brown suede sport coat in which I can imagine myself strutting. At some point I try it on and ask my parents to buy it for me. My father makes good money as the superintendent of Montgomery Millwork but this coat is a luxury item and he and my mother just laugh.

We visit in every season but winter impresses me most. I am cold with nothing to do but walk up and down in front of the stores. I feel removed when the Christmas decorations and the cheery people come out.

Since we stay on the one street it is easy to keep track of one another. For instance, all I have to do was look across the street and see my mother and sister disappear into a clothing shop or look down the street and see my father appear out of a men's store with a package under his arm. In the same way they can see me lumbering along and yell or gesture when it is time to go.

Albemarle is a more complicated town in my interior film. It has four streets connected in a grid. The color is sepia. Besides clothing stores, there is a drug store snack shop and a movie theater.

It is summer. I go to the movie theater while the others are off doing something else. A girl with long blonde hair sits in front of me. Somehow we are talking. Her hair spills over the back of her seat. I am touching her hair. Then I am sitting beside her with my arm around her shoulders. We make vague plans to stay in touch but nothing comes of it.

It is still summer, but Saturday night, not Saturday afternoon. All of us go to a movie. We have been doing this as long as I can

remember and usually I like it although dark pictures with
Barbara Stanwyck and Joan Crawford scared me when I was
little, especially when the women were crazy killers. This movie
is a musical. On the way back to Troy from my dark corner in
the backseat I hear my mother up front singing, "Deep purple…".
She never sings but tonight her voice is throaty and nice.

Sunday Afternoons

Little mythic moments…

Sunday afternoons started with Sunday mornings, which, in Troy, meant going to the Methodist Church. In 1954, and for several more years, until either depression or reflection took hold, I didn't mind. I even put on a purple robe and sang in the choir, pretending that I could read music by pitching my voice higher when the notes went up on the page and lower when the notes went down. Of course, I didn't sing too often in public because such singing required smiling and even then a smile held too long was painful.

Sunday lunch (or, as it was known then, Sunday "dinner") followed Sunday morning in the progression toward Sunday afternoon. In Troy, and in Shelby before that, this was often home-cooked fried chicken. My mother sometimes left church after Sunday school so that by the time my father, sister and I got home, the chicken, mashed potatoes, green beans, and loaf-sized biscuits would be on the table. Later, after we moved to West Palm Beach and my step-mother joined us, lunches were typically at Howard Johnson's. We discovered that my father, who claimed to have once consumed maggoty bread in the Navy when he was hungry, had been bored with fried chicken all along. He said that he had eaten it every day growing up on the farm, even, he noted, at six in the morning, cold with a biscuit, before he, his father and brothers and Big Jim, the black man, went out into the field (although he added, they usually came in at eight for a proper breakfast of eggs and country ham).

After these preliminaries, Sunday afternoons happened when we got in the car and went for a ride. We didn't go every Sunday, but we went often enough so that now it seems like every Sunday.

I don't recall any discussion about where we went. Perhaps my father selected a destination beforehand; perhaps he just drove, trying never to repeat the same route. I know that my sister and I had nothing to do with it. Nor did my grandmother when she was living with us. She was a sweet woman, so self-effacing that she sometimes seemed to disappear, although by this time Alzheimer's was making her more noticeable. Before being called "Grandmother", she was called "Mother Jane" to distinguish her from my grandfather's first wife whose name I never knew. I don't expect that my mother cared where we went so long as we went.

Only a few of the destinations stand out now.

Once we ended up in Pinehurst, the golf resort. Viewed from the Ford's windows, it was like a movie - very neat with a lot of large pine trees, big hotels, little shops, and smart people in golf togs. I don't know how my parents reacted to this place – with idle curiosity or something else. My father never held a golf club in his life. However he did like fancy hotels and room service. Perhaps that is what he imagined when driving though Pinehurst. My mother dropped out of high school to support her younger brothers and never stayed in a fancy hotel. She sometimes said we were poor even when we weren't. Maybe she commented about the well-dressed rich people; maybe she just smiled with pursed lips, confirmed in her secret resentments.

Another time we ventured on the grounds of what my parents said was a girl's correctional institution. It was winter. The trees were bare and the buildings were unadorned brick. I was excited at the prospect of seeing bad girls but the few girls I saw wandering around the sparse grounds looked sad and defensive – staring back at me as I stared at them. This visit probably prompted discussions of those relatives on my mother's side who had spent time in similar institutions, but who had, according to family lore, profited by the experience and turned out pretty good.

We often just drove along back country roads. My father still liked to look at farms and farms animals. Sometimes going by a field of pigs he slowed down so much that my mother yelled at him. He didn't care; his eyes remained on the animals. Before moving from the farm near Shelby we had owned a pig. Walking by its pen, I could hear it snuffling and grunting, but I never looked at it. I knew what was going to happen. However my father talked to the pig in affectionate tones and patted its rump, perhaps thinking of country hams hanging in the dark from the rafters of his father's curing shed.

The best trip was going down a back country road looking for mistletoe. It was one of those little moments of childhood when things just come together, like a pretty poem with no special significance. We were driving through woods down a narrow twisting road. The countryside opened up into a field. The mistletoe appeared just as the woods closed in again. It was high in an oak, a solitary patch of green dangling from a spidery pattern of black limbs against a silver sky. We gathered outside of the car to take a better look. The air wasn't so much cold as crisp. People laughed. I don't remember what happened after that. I might have had my shotgun and tried to shoot the mistletoe out of the tree. Or maybe it was never our intent to get mistletoe, but just to look at some and then return home.

Light

Light was an issue in West Palm Beach…

The first thing I noticed when getting off the bus where my 12-year-old sister and I had spent the last 20 hours in relative silence was how bright things seemed. The terminal, an ornate Mediterranean-style structure not far from the West Palm Beach yacht basin glowed white hot. It was as if my pupils had been dilated. Everything seemed sharp, like a photograph with too much contrast. (I never asked my sister about this, even years later after we became friends and, of course, it is too late now.)

It still seemed bright when I started Palm Beach High. The school complex, which included the junior high where my sister attended appeared Moorish. It occupied the entire sun-drenched crest of the only hill in that part of Florida. From the library at the top of the tallest building you could just see across West Palm and Palm Beach to a sliver of blue-green ocean. Palm trees decorated the lawn which swept down to the low stucco wall that went alongside the road in front of the school.

At lunch, I usually joined students sitting along the wall. We strolled between slow-moving cars and motorcycles to purchase subs from curt women in hairnets who worked in the little shop across the road. One day the motorcycle guys joined in a procession. They sat erect and looked straight ahead, ignoring the mostly admiring glances from the people on the wall. This temporary gang included an English boy wearing tweed and an Italian greaser in a black leather jacket. Until coming to this place I had never eaten a sub nor seen a real greaser.

It was on this wall that I argued religion with Fred. He and I had an English class together. He was fat, wore glasses, had a large head, and claimed to be an atheist. I do not remember the arguments. Possibly Fred put forth the Argument From Evil (e.g., the presence of evil indicates that an omnipotent God is either malign or indifferent – or that God is impotent and benign or simply that God doesn't exist). I can't imagine what points I might have made – maybe that the existence of the universe implies a creator. However I do remember that after a short period of time I no longer believed in God and Fred said he did. I cannot vouch for his conversion. In my case, unbelief was where I had been heading all my life.

After losing faith (but only incidentally because of that) the world got darker. It was as if I had put on tinted glasses.

The transition was preceded by a revelation which was prompted by a party.

I was invited to parties because of my resemblance to James Dean. This one was in a banquet hall by the ocean. I probably drifted around the edges of the crowd, talked to a few people, then left early. On my way out, I encountered Mary, a girl from school. She was standing at the top of a stairway overlooking the water. As I recall, the building was cream colored; the surf splashed, and the moon danced on the waves. We talked a little, joking about her unpronounceable Slovak name. I revealed my unbelief, suggesting there is nothing there. She didn't see things that way but was sympathetic and asked me to come back in with her. I wanted to but could not even see the possibility of saying yes.

I drove back down A1A in my father's rust-pitted 50 Ford, past empty mansions on the left and the ocean on the right. I thought about there being nothing there. Something opened up. I stood over a void in which all my reasons and restrictions fell. I was without meaning, free.

I looked at the ocean. The moon, as it does, seemed to follow me. Then I shifted my attention and tried to think about something else.

French Words

Pidawee dreams of social grandeur...

I learned about French words when I was at Palm Beach Junior College. That was in 1957, a year after we moved to West Palm Beach and almost two years after my mother died. The school was new, a collection of contemporary buildings which today would look like a strip mall. I don't think William Calley (who would later lead the killings at My Lai) was there yet. But maybe he was and I just didn't notice him because he was so ordinary looking. I don't suppose I was ordinary looking because people said I was a dead ringer for James Dean, which seemed to attract girls, at least until they got to know me.

The first French word was "gauche". It was spoken by a beautiful Jewish girl who sat in the back of my English class. She was thin and imperious, with long black hair, which glistened, as they said in the historical novels that I read, like a raven's wing. I don't remember the context but I remember the word, uttered in a slightly nasal tone, the vowels drawn out like salt-water taffy – "gooohhhsh".

I was hooked. I realized (at a non-verbal level where all of my awareness resided) that the key to beautiful Jewish girls was being able to say words like gauche. Such abilities might help me become a beatnik and even someday a Southern Writer in New York. It had been that way in Shelby, where access to certain religious circles depended on the ability to say "Juh-e-sus" with three syllables. Until Florida, I had sought Jesus and salvation, embarrassing my friends at Young Life, asking what it meant to be saved.

Of course, I soon discovered that the term gauche actually referred to me, and that I must be able to speak and possibly even understand other French and associated words.

There was Sartre, spoken as "Sahharrt!". I learned that he was fat and ugly and the inventor of existentialism. I tried reading the "The Age of Reason" but could not finish it.

There was also Camus, pronounced "Camooooo". I learned that he was better looking and the popularizer of absurdity. I read "The Stranger" and identified with Meursault the alienated killer.

I discovered that absurd was pronounced "absssuurrd", even though it wasn't French. Perhaps I overheard this when I was hanging upside down from the awning in the front of the Palm Beach Bath and Tennis Club and George Hamilton, who would later become an actor, walked underneath, responding to my greeting, "George" with a pleasant enough, "Tom". But I knew what absurdity was and did not have to finish "The Myth of Sisyphus" to find out.

Even though I once sat in a coffee shop and wrote poetry on the back of a napkin, I never did figure out existentialism. When I asked HT, my one real beatnik friend, who had a bongo drum and a monkey skin rug in her room, she just laughed. When I asked the beautiful Jewish girl she muttered something about existence preceding essence and walked off.

It is surprising, but the word ennui did not come up in Florida; although it would after we returned to Shelby. I am reminded of ennui by the episode of Star Trek where Spock returns to Vulcan with Kirk, Doc and the others to get married so that he may have sex and avoid death. An old woman who looks like a Hungarian Jewess and wears what appears to be a Hindu headdress leads the ceremony. Spock (or Kirk, as Spock's champion) is challenged to a fight and the old woman says that it has something to do with the "onwooh" - which sounds like ennui.

Angst possibly also came up in Florida. But it is a German word with only French association.

Racing Around West Palm Beach

Unlike racing in Shelby, racing in West Palm Beach was solitary...

I raced mostly in the vicinity of the Air Force base near where we lived (and where two planes crashed, a B-25 and C-130 as I recall – although that is another story). The roads were especially good in the rain because the impermeable pavement of asphalt and seashells promoted hydroplaning. Going around the curve at the end of the runway where I once saw the Blue Angels roar low overheard then abruptly lift toward heaven it didn't require much throttle to make the rear end of the old Ford creep out toward the jungle on the side of the road.

I raced in whatever vehicle was handy.

When my step-mother came to live with us, I raced her pretty blue 53 Chevrolet coupe. It was sold to her and maintained by Crawley, her brother-in-law, who was the Chevrolet dealer in Shelby. He had bulldog jowls like J. Edgar Hoover and when drinking encouraged his Chihuahua to sing. I took her Chevrolet out on back roads behind the base, pushed the gas pedal to the floor then let the clutch pop. The knobby snow tires that Crawley had installed did not squeal but just gnawed at the odd aggregate until the car gained traction and lurched off.

When my father traded the old Ford for a fancy white 1957 Chevrolet Bel Aire hard top, I raced that too. I drove it on the same back roads and when the car was going as fast as it could go, floating lightly over the wavy pavement at 110 MPH, I slammed on the brakes. The tires squealed and the car nosed down like a horse whose reins had been jerked. I did this repeatedly until the brakes got hot and failed. I called it high-speed braking practice.

Although my solitary racing usually had no affect on other people, there were a few exceptions.

I once wrecked the Chevrolet - although it wasn't strictly racing. At a traffic light between West Palm Beach and Palm Beach, I ran into the back of a Willys Jeepster. I had shifted my eyes to the car lot on the side of the road to admire a swooping old convertible which I knew from Road and Track magazines was a Delahaye. The hitch protruding from the back of the Jeepster punctured the Chevrolet's grill. My father didn't get mad, never got really mad at me and I made no connection between that man and the man who reportedly had bashed a would-be bandit in the head with a tire iron one night in 1928 on the way back from Tijuana and who had been asked by Jack Legs Diamond in 1931 to join his organization as a collector.

There was the incident with Rose. I had been invited to a party at a private home in Palm Beach. I suppose it was again my James Dean resemblance. I drove up in the old, rust-pitted Ford in the early evening, when shadows of palms fluttered against the white stucco of the rambling, single-story structure. Inside, it was all muted lighting and soft pastels. The hosts were well-dressed, generous and kind. Rose was exquisite. I got the impression she did not quite belong there either, although she belonged more than me. She sat across from me in a big overstuffed chair, her perfectly tanned legs tucked up under yellow shorts. We talked. I don't remember what we said, but the tone, on my side anyway, seemed unstoppably grandiose. Later, somebody suggested that I drive her home. She sat curled across from me on the front seat, her smooth knees pointing at my face. I suppose I did it to impress her. Going back North on A1A there was a tight curve that I had learned to slide around. So, that is what I did. She didn't have time to prepare. One moment we were driving along and the next moment we were roaring around this curve, maybe about to die. She recovered quickly enough and turned away but I had seen the fear of me make her ugly.

There was also the thing at Graham Eckes private school. It was on the other end of Palm Beach island, not far, I think, from the Kennedy house and not far from a driveway with a large mirror turned to reveal oncoming traffic. I was driving the old Ford. The students, like large birds in their blue uniforms, were crossing the road. I don't think I came close to hitting anybody. But there was a dithering flutter of activity and I did slam on the brakes. Since this was the only way out, I waited behind the abutment at the end of the island for an hour or so before venturing back down A1A toward the bridge that went to West Palm Beach.

This was perhaps the day that I imagined the Ford and I were stationary and Palm Beach was actually moving past us. The idea came from a book about relativity. I had played with the notion before, but on that day, I might have actually altered my perception enough to scare myself.

George Hamilton

A successful pidawee...

Over the years I have maintained a proprietary interest in George Hamilton.

In the 60's, when he was dating Linda Bird Johnson and I was a technician at Celanese wearing a green shirt with a badge that said "Tom", I took some satisfaction in being only a few degrees of separation from power. I had encountered George; George had gone out with Linda, and Linda was the daughter of Lyndon – who as President had come close in 1964 to activating the Army Reserves and sending me to Vietnam.

In the 70's, after I quit inventing building systems and space ships to write unsold novels, I considered (and might have actually tried) contacting George to help me promote my work.

Later, when George became known primarily for his tan, I felt sorry for him until I realized that my pity might be misplaced.

At the time of this writing my wife and I watch him on a dance show and make statements like, "Well, old George is still looking pretty good." I like seeing him cavort with an attractive young woman who is as sleek as a seal.

Although I have dropped George into many conversations, there wasn't much of a connection (which I always note with coy, self-deprecating modesty).

The first connection was sartorial. At Palm Beach High in 1956-57, I think that George and I were among the few boys to wear sport coats. Everybody else adopted a more casual style.

George appeared in the annual in his sport coat. It was plaid –
green and blue as I recall. My coat, purchased in West Palm
Beach from a little man who told me that I looked tasteful, was
the color of brushed aluminum. I wore it on a visit back to
Shelby and when I went by the Silver Villa drive-in, Charles, who
later became an attorney, made some comment about me being
"Palm Beach Tom".

The second connection was as Hollywood look-alikes. It was
noted in the school newspaper that George looked like Tony
Perkins and I looked like James Dean. I always thought that my
resemblance was more legitimate.

We actually talked only twice.

Once was out by the wall in front of the school where he had
parked his Kaiser Darren sports car. Everybody was aware of
the car with its long graceful lines and odd smug grill. On that
day it would not crank and I found myself with a group of boys
trying to figure out what was wrong. George proclaimed no
mechanical expertise and stood back while we lifted the hood
and pontificated. Up close the plastic body seemed cheap and
the six-cylinder Willys engine was unimpressive. No one solved
the problem, at least while I was standing there.

The other time we talked was somewhere in Palm Beach. It
was probably the Bath and Tennis Club because I knew HT, the
beatnik girl, who knew the son of the caretaker and I got invited
to parties there during the off season when no members were
present. I don't remember now why I was hanging from the
entrance awning frame. Perhaps I had chinned a cross member
and because that felt good had swung myself on over to hang by
the back of my knees. I know that I wasn't embarrassed and
when George passed under the awning on his way into the
building I said, "George" and he smiled, and said, "Tom".

If George dies before me, and if I have my wits about me, I look
forward to telling how I knew him before we got old.

Yankee Girls

Pidawee adventures...

That we were not yet deep thinkers was demonstrated on a daily basis, but some occasions stand out, like rites of passage in a peculiar religion.

For instance, there was the time in the old graphite mine.

I don't know who suggested the trip. I found myself in a car going out of Shelby, past the McKinney farm with the big house and the horse stables, past the smaller house, fallen in then, where my grandfather had been a tenant farmer on land owned by his aunt, past a bridge over a small creek. When we pulled off the side of the road, there were no houses, just a field and some wooded hills.

Only one person knew where the mine was located. We followed, eight or nine of us more-or-less single file, across the field and into the woods. We chattered and laughed while pushing through undergrowth, dodging briars, and stepping over or under old barbed wire grown into the sides of living trees. Sensing some confusion on the part of our leader, several wondered if he was lost. But after climbing a hill that didn't look any different from the hills already climbed, we came to a hole, about eight feet high, in the side of a slope. Heavy thickets grew up to the edge of the opening. It looked like the entrance to a natural cave, or a womb – or a tomb.

Entering the cave, we went along a horizontal shaft maybe 100 feet then climbed down an old ladder in a vertical shaft a dozen feet or so to another level. I recall that there was always light. I don't know if someone brought a flashlight or if the second level opened to the outside. Other than the ladder and the tunnel itself, there was no evidence of human activity. It was only years later that I learned that my father had worked in the mine in 1914, when he was a boy.

Until Doane did what he did I wasn't afraid. The clay walls and roof seemed secure. I think I was on the lower level, when I heard him yell out in a dramatic voice, "I am going to set off ultrasonic vibrations and kill us all. He! He!" Then he fired a pistol several times. Although it was only a little .25 automatic, it sounded like a cannon inside that confined space. I recall smelling the gunpowder, feeling the tunnel close in and resenting the people who were between me and the entrance.

Outside when asked why he did it, Doane just laughed.

Two other occasions that illustrate our status as proto-thinkers involved statements made by Toby (who might have been on the trip to the graphite mine and might have been the one who questioned Doane).

Toby claims that he didn't make one of the statements. I asked him about it years later when we were sitting in front of the Dairy Queen drinking coffee. It was during one of his periodic visits from Missouri where he had settled after getting out of the Army in the early 60's. Children played near, but not in, the parking lot. Wives and friends chatted around the long outdoor table. Toby reflected for a moment, then announced no, he hadn't said it, and implied by his manner that it was not something so bad that he would have to lie about it. But I distinctly remember being at another hang-out, maybe 40 years earlier. I can still sense someone leaning over, speaking in that same whisper, saying how we could or should (that part I am not sure about) hide on a hill overlooking the road going out of town and shoot the tires out from under the bus that was taking home the opposing team (basketball I think). The idea, as I recall, was not to cause death or injury, simply inconvenience. Of course it was just talk, like all the rest of our talk.

There is no disagreement about the other statement. Toby remembers it. I suppose Doane does too, although I don't talk to him often. He's retired and living in Providence, Rhode Island where he once worked as an investigative reporter.

It was 1958 or 1959. Ft. Lauderdale had become a destination for young people on spring break. Toby was at Gardner Webb College near Shelby; Doane was at Chapel Hill, and I was at Palm Beach Junior College.

Toby and Doane decided that it would be a good thing to come see me then go down to Ft. Lauderdale and look for Yankee Girls Gone Wild. Neither Toby nor Doane had a car so they went to a junk yard and bought a 1948, four-door Nash – for $75 I think. Legend has it that the dealer threw in three or four mismatched tires in case there was a flat. In today's terms, the car would be the size of a large SUV.

Like Max going to see the Wild Things, Toby and Doane drove through a night and a day to my house in West Palm Beach, in a little subdivision near the dog track, out near the Air Force base. Then we went on down to Ft. Lauderdale.

My memories of the day are fragmentary. Parking the Nash out of view, we joined the other young people who roamed the streets and the beach. It was odd, but although they were from all over the east coast, most seemed to know one another - or at least to be a part of a larger group, who recognized, without being told, other members of the group.

It was clear that we were not members. This message was delivered by the Yankee Girls Gone Wild when they failed to respond to our clever repartee. It was reinforced by the surly operators of beach-front establishments who seemed more rude to us than to the others who stood in the long lines.

At some point in the afternoon, it was decided that we should move on south toward Miami.

The shining moment, the moment that we will all remember, occurred as we were driving out of town. At a signal light, in the middle of traffic, something happened to the Nash. A noise came from the front end and the engine started to shake. Raising the tomb-like hood, we discovered that one of the fan blades was either off or about to come off (I don't remember which). Although the object of amused looks from the Yankee Girls Gone Wild, and perhaps even being yelled at by the police, somebody, probably Toby, had an inspiration. The engine was vibrating because the fan was dynamically unbalanced. That was the only thing stopping us from leaving – the possibility that the engine would shake itself apart. However, if we broke off one blade, that would leave two blades opposite each other. The assembly would be balanced. Right then it didn't make any difference if the engine melted on down the road. We would at least be away from this place of shame. So one of us, again, probably Toby, pulled off a fan blade. As predicted, the engine vibration stopped.

The memorable phrase was voiced as we started to drive away. Toby stuck his head out the window of the Nash and yelled, as loud as he could, "YANKEE GIRLS EAT SHIT!."

I don't remember anything that happened after that. I don't know if we went on to Miami or just turned around and went back to West Palm Beach. I did hear that the Nash, with just two fan blades, got Toby and Doane back to Shelby and that the last anyone heard was still running.

Re-visiting history...

HT was a real beatnik. Today she is probably a grandmother. Biologically, she could even be a great-grandmother – if her child, who would be 45 now, had a child at age 20 (which is when HT became a mother) and that child also had a child at 20.

The last time I saw her was January, 1961 when I returned to West Palm Beach with Frank, Bill, and Coleman. It was one of those trips that unmarried friends take on the spur of the moment, but married friends plan or don't take at all. We rode down in Frank's prim little Fiat sedan. There was some ice on the ground when we left Shelby but by Daytona Beach, we lowered the windows, and by West Palm Beach we put on short sleeves.

Although I had not been in touch with HT since before we left West Palm Beach two years earlier, I called her soon after we arrived. My plan was to take her out and thereby suggest to my friends that there had been something between us - that I had a girl during those lost years in Florida. Her younger sister, Dodson Aphrodite ("Dottie") answered the phone. She said that HT wasn't there anymore – that she had married a local radio personality, had a baby, and was now living down near Lake Worth.

Figuring that Dottie at 17 was even more impressive than Dottie at 15 I asked her if she wanted to go out. She said sure.

I then blew a half week's salary renting a British racing green Triumph roadster (that was so low you could touch the pavement without opening the door) and drove past old haunts, still alone, but now in a better car.

I went past Palm Beach High where I had first met HT, five years earlier. I had not been in the school more than a few months and was walking from science class to the main building, up the only hill in this part of Florida, when someone tugged at my shirt and said, "Mister."

Turning around, ready either to fawn or fight, I encountered a plump pretty girl (zoftig might be the word) with short black hair and a suggestive grin. She said, "Can I have your autograph?"

I mumbled, "What?"

She laughed, "You're James Dean aren't you?"

I mumbled, "Ah."

Still smiling, but now in the fixed manner of someone finishing a job that should perhaps never have been started, she went on to tell me that there was going to be a party at her place and would I like to go. I said I would.

I went to maybe four parties over the next couple years either because HT asked me or got somebody to ask me.

Most were at HT's place. It was a duplex apartment in an older part of West Palm Beach with Mediterranean style houses that dated back to the 20's or 30's. There were a lot of trees, big oaks and Australian pines. Everything seemed dark and heavy. HT lived with her sister and mother and sometimes her mother's boyfriend, whose name might have been Hayes.

The apartment had posters on the wall, perhaps a yellow one with Miles Davis, leaning back like a matador, blowing his trumpet at a bull and another one with Jack Kerouac, smoking a cigarette. The furniture was old and overstuffed with pillows on the hardwood floor. There was a bongo drum in the corner and a brown and white monkey skin rug in HT's bedroom. Everything was slightly cluttered.

HT made dramatic entrances, said clever things and orchestrated people in a nice way. Her mother was a dark Greek whom HT treated more like an older sister than a mother. Dottie looked like her mother. All the people around HT seemed clever and sophisticated. Several could actually play the bongo drum. Most were tolerant of the one they referred to both as James Dean and Little Abner.

I recall two parties that were not at HT's apartment. One was at the house of the boy whose father worked for the Palm Beach Bath and Tennis club. We crowded into his bedroom and listened to the Sounds Of Le Mans played on his new hi fi, marveling at how the racing car noises started in one corner of the room and moved to another corner, making you think you were actually there, maybe rubbing shoulders with Jean Paul – assuming he went to those things.

The other party was in a less affluent part of town. We drank beer in the back yard and listened to a Jewish boy talk about stealing milk and newspapers from his neighbors. This struck me as odd because the few Jews in Shelby were well off and that's how I assumed all Jews lived. When I left early, HT asked me for a ride home. It occurs to me now that she might have actually wanted to be alone with me. We stopped in a bleak all-night drive-in to get coffee because I was concerned about being drunk. I brought the coffee out to the car where HT sat propped against the door. We tried talking but I couldn't think of anything to say and we left.

After that she moved to Puerto Rico to go to school or to do good work; I don't remember. I got one letter from a place called Saint something or other.

I did not see her again until Dottie and I drove up in my British racing green Triumph.

My only real image is of the three of us standing in a room; HT at one end; Dottie in the middle and me at the other end. We are frozen in the moment. HT says I seem different. Somebody comments about the passage of time and how the two sisters are also different – one with a family now, the other recently grown up. I blurt out something about making mad passionate love to the sister that is available. This makes HT cringe which makes me cringe but Dottie seems to think it is amusing.

The rest is inferred and imagined. We certainly looked at the apartment; my impression now is that it was neat and attractively decorated. I think we met the radio personality husband; I recall that he was an ass (or maybe I am remembering some other personality encountered in later years). We looked at the baby (and again, maybe I am remembering another pastel room and another small crib).

Then after a while, we left.

I took Dottie out two more times. She tried to find dates for my companions but no one among her friends was interested. I think Bill must have seen her because a lifetime later he still talks about the dark sexy girl.

One night, after leaving Dottie, I went bar-hopping with Joe, in whose apartment we were staying. I drank martinis on top of cheap wine and got very sick. Looking out from the bathroom where I was kneeling in front of the commode, the window seemed to slowly close, then pop open, then close again. Seeing me, Frank said, "Tee hee; Tom's sick."

At the end of the week, Frank, Coleman, Bill and I squeezed back in the Fiat and returned to Shelby. The trip took 21 hours because of detours to towns where Coleman knew girls who were not in when we came by. To pass the time, we played chess on a little peg board set loaned to us by Larry. Coleman and I played a game that lasted through the central part of Florida. I lost, but it was still the best game of my life.

PRE-HISTORY

1901 – 1954

Asheville

Phenix City

Shelby

San Diego

New York

Honolulu

Tijuana

Molly and B.K.

Imagining an episode with Molly and BK...

Getting the pictures made was B.K.'s idea. Molly didn't want to, saying she was "too ugly".

The photographer's studio was located on the second floor of a red brick building just off main street. Across the hall was a doctor's office. Downstairs was a drug store and soda shop.

Molly and B.K lived in a little house on the edge of town, beyond where the road turned from asphalt to gravel. The house was constructed during the town's latest growth spurt. There were two bedrooms, a kitchen, and a living room, with a hallway down the middle. They had not accumulated much yet, just a table, several chairs, an iron-frame bed painted white, a sofa, and a chest. In their bedroom, B.K. had attached pegs to the wall to hang clothes, sanding the pegs smooth so they wouldn't snag the fabric.

Just beyond the back door was a well house and 100 feet beyond that at the end of a path through the weeds was a one-hole privy. In the spring, blue bonnets grew beside the path. Sometimes B.K. picked a handful and gave them to Molly to put in a coffee can with water. Sometimes, she picked flowers and sometimes she kicked at them with the toe of her black, lace-up shoe.

The house still smelled like newly cut pine. B.K. was a lumberman and liked the smell. The odor made Molly sick although the earthy scent of the privy didn't especially bother her. When it wasn't too hot or cold sometimes she just sat there, reading a book or the newspaper.

They had been married two years when the picture was made. They moved here for the job that B.K. got managing the saw mill. Both of their families still lived in the mountains. By this time she had already lost one child, a boy, whom they buried in a grave marked with a rock. B.K. visited the grave a few times. Molly went with him once then refused whenever he brought it up. Molly thought about babies when she sat in the privy, poised over the hole.

They dressed in their most stylish clothes and walked the half mile from their house to the studio. There was no sidewalk until they got to the part of the road that was paved. B.K. commented about the big houses that sat back from the sidewalk on well-tended lawns. He especially liked the Mediterranean style mansion with the child-sized cottage in the front yard. Molly noted that it was nicer than the little house where they lived and wondered if the rich people would rent it to them – but then went on to say they probably wouldn't want a family of hillbillies living in their front yard. .

It was July so at B.K.'s insistence they stopped at the soda shop before going upstairs to the studio. Both had orangeades over shaved ice. They sat at a little table under the ceiling fan letting the evaporating sweat cool them off. B.K. talked about his work, wondering how long it would last, and Molly nodded from time to time and stared out of the window at the bleached summer afternoon. Finally she turned to the big Ingersoll clock ticking on the wall behind the counter and said, "Well, let's go on."

The stairwell was dark and steep. Halfway up Molly felt a pain in her abdomen and wondered if she was pregnant again. She made herself keep up with B.K. and was breathing hard when they got to the top.

The photographer greeted them at the door. He was a grinning thin man with red veined cheeks and a soiled tie. Molly had heard from a woman in the Methodist church that he was a drunk. When Molly told B.K., he had said, "Well, he can probably still take good pictures."

Molly brushed her hair and B.K. put on the coat that he had been carrying over his arm. The man tried to get Molly to smile but she wouldn't do it and finally he just stopped and took the picture. The flash powder exploding on the tray in the darkened room left her momentarily blinded. She thought, but didn't say, that it smelled hellish, like hell.

After the session was over and they had walked back down into the glare of the street, B.K. told Molly that he had something to do and why didn't she go on home. She didn't ask him what, knowing that he wanted to go to the bar. She walked away, feeling the heat bake into soles of her shoes, looking forward to the shade, thinking that she might bring it up later.

Molly and Eva

Imagining little stories that Molly might have told to Eva...

One winter night in the big house in Asheville, sitting before the fireplace, her voice mixing with the whisper of the wind and rain, Molly told Eva about the Tweeds.

"They lived in a castle in Scotland." The curtain rustled and Molly glanced at the window. Her watery reflection stared back. "It was cold and rainy there too."

"They were our relatives?"

"Umhm."

"But they are dead now?"

"Yes. That was a long time ago."

"What did they do in Scotland?"

Molly pretended to concentrate. "Well, the lords fought a lot."

"Who did they fight?"

"They fought everybody - each another, the English, before that the Romans, who built a wall to keep them out."

Eva frowned. "I think the lords were bad men."

Molly nodded, "I suppose.", then she smiled, her face flickering red in the firelight. "But do you know what?"

"What?"

"They wore dresses."

Eva giggled. "Like girls wear?"

"Yes, but different. They called them kilts."

"Did they wear bloomers?"

"I don't think so."

Eva made a face. "They must have gotten cold. Why did they fight so much?"

Molly laughed. Her voice was a sweet contralto. "Because their pidawees were freezing off."

Eva snickered. "What did the ladies do?"

"They had the babies."

"What did they do after that?"

The fire popped. Eva jumped a little.

Molly idly stroked her daughter's hair. "I don't know sweetie. I suppose they just died."

* * * * *

One summer evening, after eating homemade peach ice cream that Molly had mixed and B.K. had churned, and everybody was sitting on blankets in the front yard and looking up at the stars, Eva leaned back against her mother's bosom, and said, "Tell me a story."

Molly said, "No, baby, I'm tired. Lie still."

"Please."

Molly sighed and adjusted her position. "All right. It seems that there was once a Parris who got himself hung."

Eva wiggled. "With a rope around his neck?"

"Yes mam."

"Why?"

"He was a pirate. They hung him on Parris Island, where they hung all the pirates back then."

"Was it named after us, this island?"

Her father's voice answered from the dark, "Maybe."

Eva leaned back and looked up at her mother's pale face. "Was he a bad man?"

Molly buried her nose in the tart smell of her daughter's hair and laughed. "Why no, sweetie, not according to the story your grandmother told. He was what they called a privateer. That means he was like a soldier fighting in a war. He was just unlucky."

"That's too bad."

"Yes, isn't it."

* * * * *

One spring day, Molly and Eva were weeding the little garden behind the house. Molly used a hoe, methodically chopping up and down. Eva walked behind, tugging at the plants her mother had loosened. It was already hot and both mother and daughter were sweating. Molly, who was usually pregnant, was pregnant again.

She stopped, leaned against the hoe and said, "Damn. If I was a Parris man, I think I'd switch sides about now."

Eva looked up at her mother's swollen body.

"That's what they did back in the Civil War. When things got tough the men switched sides. For instance like right now, during planting time, the men that didn't want to work might join one side or the other. Then when they were ready to work they'd just leave and come home."

Eva wiped her hands on her dress, leaving red clay streaks, like dried blood. "When it was time to pick what was planted?"

"Sure, then."

"What did the women do?"

"They just did."

Eva

Half-imagined stories told by Eva to me...

"We had tornadoes when I was growing up in Alabama. One Sunday morning a tornado picked up a colored church right off its foundation. It was in the middle of worship and the church was full of people all dressed up in their Sunday best with the women wearing big fancy hats and the men in suits or at least clean and starched high-back overalls and white shirts. The tornado turned the church around once and set it back down but facing the other way now with the front where the back used to be. It didn't break a thing, not even the pitcher of iced tea that the preacher kept in the pulpit for when it got hot."

"What did the people do?"

She laughed her voice husky and soft like honey still on the comb. "They shouted hallelujah and kept on singing."

It was the summer. The room was close and hot. She opened the top drawer of her dresser and pulled out an old cigar box. She removed a small folding fan. It was made from thin strips of carved ivory tied together with silk strings. Some of the strings were broken and some of the ivory strips hung loose. She let her 10-year old son hold the fan. He carefully opened and closed it a few times, then tentatively waved it in front of his face, feeling the breeze, smelling powder and perfume and the faint odor of age.

"My great uncle brought this back from Alaska after the Gold Rush."

"Did he find any gold?"

"No. None of us ever got rich."

She smiled and stared at nothing. "I wanted to travel but when my mother died, I had to stay home and look after Bobby and Ken."

She talked about the reform politician, Albert Patterson, from Phenix City, Alabama, as if she might have known him. (Phenix City, which is just across the Chattahoochee River from Columbus, Georgia, had the reputation of being the most corrupt town in the United States.) My impression was that he might have helped her with a problem. In June 1954, after being elected Alabama Attorney General, Patterson was assassinated by the Phenix City crime mob. Coincidentally, next summer, Eva was diagnosed with a fatal cancer.

She talked about the dog, Rex.

"Rex was a big black German Sheppard. He loved your grandfather. He followed him everywhere, from the house to downtown and back. He'd wait out front when papa went inside somewhere, lying there till papa came out."

"One day the house caught fire. Rex kept running in and out of the house, barking, and making sure that people were safe. The last time he ran in I think he was looking for Bobby, although he was already out. We tried to stop him but he went in anyway. He didn't make it back that time. The house fell in on him."

Granny

Remembering my grandmother who at times seemed to be hardly there…

This is how my father remembered her in his memoirs:

I suppose Mother Jane was approximately 40 years old, about five feet six inches tall and weighed around 130 pounds. She had blue eyes, a fair complexion, long black hair with some gray, and a very beautiful smile that she used rather effectively. She also had a very pronounced frown whenever the occasion called for it. Of course, I am sure every five year old boy has a beautiful mother.

She never went to a movie, flew on an airplane, or drove a car.

When her husband, Issac Yancey, died she slipped into the background of other households.

Each month she got a little money from the government which she used to buy Tuberose snuff, small blue jars of Noxzema lotion, and crochet thread. She dipped the snuff with twigs whose ends she frayed like toothbrush bristles. She rubbed the Noxzema on her hands to help alleviate arthritis pains. She crocheted the thread into intricate doilies, table cloths, and bedcovers.

She even disappeared when reading stories to her grandchildren. Decades later I can only remember her disembodied voice and the tales she told. I can't see her face. It was as if the stories read themselves.

She was not a person but a presence.

I first remember her when we were living in Baltimore during the war years. I might have been four or five. She appeared from nowhere in the back yard where I was trying to hammer nails into a board. She seemed tall and stern. She offered advice about how to drive nails (probably the same advice my father offered 30 years later when I was one of his carpenters). Then she tried to straighten the nails I had bent. I remember thinking how ugly the nails had become, knowing nothing was going to make them right again. Then she disappeared back into nowhere.

When we returned to Shelby after the war, she lived with us most of the time. Finding a place to put her always seemed to be a problem. Sometimes she shared a bedroom and a bed with my sister or me. After my sister started having problems with bed wetting, Granny got her own bedroom.

I never realized that Granny might want to work until the day on Lee Street when the commode overflowed, probably as a result of something I had done. Granny grabbed a mop and started swishing up the water with large vigorous strokes, displaying strength I didn't know she had. A few minutes later my mother made a dramatic entrance, yelled something and Granny retreated back into herself.

Granny stayed in herself until she got Alzheimer's. Then she started coming out until there was nothing left inside.

The symptoms first appeared when we were living on the farm, several years before my mother died. One day Granny wandered down the dirt road that went by our house, headed for South Carolina. The young doctor sat in our living room and said in sympathetic tones that she was becoming senile, which is what most Weathers do if we live long enough.

When my mother got sick Granny went to live with Uncle Paul and stayed there until we came back from Florida with a new step-mother who could help look after things. Granny moved back in with us.

The disease had progressed in those five years. She wrapped small hard pieces of excrement in toilet paper like little ears of corn, and hid them in her dresser drawers. Although a picky eater before the disease set in, she now ate anything, including, once, a napkin that I pulled from her mouth. She repeated the phrase "Oooh, oooh I smell peaches. Here come's Johnny with a hole in his breeches." And she had imaginary conversations with someone named Lawson Botts.

Always trying to find something to brag about, I once made a comment to my girlfriend, Diane, about the memorable old lady living in our house. Diane hesitated, then screwed up her face in a pixie smile and said, "But she is so old."

A couple of years later, after my step-mother had had enough, I went with my father to take Granny to the mental institution in Morganton. It was the only place that would have her. Some doctor, as a favor to the family, must have declared her insane. She sat in the back seat and nobody said anything, not even my father.

After a month or so, we brought her back to his house. She lay in the spare bedroom for a week, unmoving, staring at the ceiling, and then was pronounced dead.

Isaac Yancey

Imagining a conversation between my father and his father...

This is how my father remembered him in his memoirs:

My dad was Isaac Yancey. He was called IY or Big Isaac by most people who knew him, so I will call him Big Isaac. He was six feet two inches tall, weighed about 210 pounds and was in his mid-forties. He had big broad shoulders, a rather small waist and hands about the size of a small country ham. He had steely blue eyes that could cut you to pieces, iron gray hair and a mustache, a ready smile or a very pronounced frown. He was a master at eating you out, or "lecturing you" as he called it, although he never hit below the belt. He had one weakness. Just before he finished talking to you and was about ready to tease or kid you, if you could look long enough into those hard blue eyes, you could maybe see a very small quiver or teasing little smile and a very small twitch in each corner of his mouth. You knew you were just about off the hook before he told you that was all for now. Once he brought up a subject he never brought it up again.

"Dad?"

It was after breakfast and the man was sitting at the big scarred kitchen table drinking another cup of coffee before going back out in the field. His wife was at the other end of the table working on biscuits for the noon meal. The colored man known as Big Jim, who ate with them at the little table in the corner of the kitchen, had already gone outside. The man wore high back overalls and rough un-tanned boots. His wife wore a faded blue dress. Her black hair, tinged with gray, was pulled into a bun although a few stray wisps clung to her neck which was already sweaty. Everybody, the man, the woman, the boy sitting with his head down at the next place, all the family, had a slightly sour smell because it was Wednesday and the big tin bathing tub would not be pulled out until Saturday night.

"What do you want boy?"

"Well, sir, I wanted to ask you a question."

The man loudly sipped his coffee, and put the cup down on the table. "The woman said, "Do you want any more?"

He said, "No thanks. I'm going back out in a minute. Just after I finish some business here."

The woman glanced at the two of them, her gaze lingering on the boy, then went back to the biscuit dough she was kneading in the large wooden bowl.

The man said to the boy, "All right. But look at me when you talk. I've told you that before."

The boy sat up so that his entire spine was in contact with the back of the cane chair, which squeaked a little with his movement. He lifted his head and looked at the man. "Yes sir."

"Well?"

"It's about Big Jim."

"What about him?" The man's voice took on a different tone.

The boy's voice shook, but his gaze did not waver. "How come he eats at the little table and we eat over here at the big table? There's room for him over here."

The woman, both hands wrapped around a big ball of dough, stopped to listen.

The man said, "Ah, that. You've been asking me about that for the past year and I've told you that's just the way it is. Niggers just don't sit at the same table as white people." He paused. "Anyway, if I did ask Jim to come over and sit with us it would embarrass him."

The boy stuck his chin out, holding the man's gaze. "I know. That's what you told me. But I eat with Jim and Hattie and Gus at their table at their house."

The man looked down briefly then looked back. "That's different. They don't mind. Anyway, you're still a boy."

The boy said, "Well, I don't see...."

The man slid his chair back, which scraped across the uneven wooden floor. "All right. It's time for work. You go help Jim."

The boy, still holding the man's gaze said, "Yes sir."

* * * * * *

Twenty years later, returning home from his first leave in the Navy, the boy, now a man, walked up from the edge of the gravel road where the cab had let him out. He carried a duffle bag lightly over his shoulder. There was no one outside but he could smell cooking from the kitchen at the back of the house. He pulled open the screen door and saw a group sitting at the long table. At first he wasn't sure who they were because the room was dark after coming in from the light and some of the people appeared dark. He thought he might be in the wrong house. Then the large man at the end of the table, said, "Well just don't stand there boy, come on in."

The other large man got up from his place, which has been the boy's place, walked past Hattie and Gus, the two other black people at the big table, grabbed the boy's bicep with one large hand and said, "Well look at you Tom. Just look at you."

Tom in Navy

Recalling conversations with my father about his time in the Navy in the 1920's...

"...and before going in the Navy I went to see Mr. Lutz with my share of the cotton money and ordered a new suit (because I had a 48 inch chest and a 30 inch waist and regular store-bought clothes didn't fit). I figured the suit would get me noticed and I'd be put in charge of the other recruits on the train trip from Charlotte to the naval training station in Norfolk, not only to tell them what to do but to take care the meal money on the way so that if nobody asked when we arrived (which they didn't) I could keep what was left over (which I did)."

"... and I was walking down a street in San Diego with a girl on each arm. A third girl who was with us tipped my cap back on my head at a cocky angle when two shore police came up and one pointed his night stick in my face and yelled, "Sailor straighten up that damn hat". I laughed and he swung at me with the night stick. I pulled my left arm loose from the girl on that side and he hit it and damn it hurt but I got a right hook in his face and blood flew everywhere over him and me. Somebody grabbed me from behind and I spun around and hit him on the chin before seeing who it was and he went down. When I saw, oh damn, it was a Junior Lieutenant I apologized and helped him get up but they took me to jail anyway."

"... and when we were docked in New York I saw the old man sneak a woman into his cabin. I didn't say anything to anybody but I made sure that he knew I knew."

"...and I was walking down an off-limits street in Panama City with Jim and Ski wearing civilian clothes without permission without papers looking for three of our guys who had not come back from shore leave. We were all scared because it was a bad place where you had to watch out for robbers and the police. Finally we found some teenagers who spoke English who told us that three sailors in uniform were down the street in a house. After some discussion I got stuck with seeing what was going on while Jim and Ski stayed behind. I told them if I didn't show up I would be in jail and to get Mister Mason and come back with the 700 dollars poker money I had hidden in my locker. And sure enough it was our guys drunk and arguing with a whore about 100 dollars one of them said she stole and I told them let's get the hell out of here. Then the stupid sonofabitch hit her and you could have heard her yelling all over town and four Panama cops showed up. I managed to knock two of them down before they swarmed over me. I spent the weekend in the Panama City jail until Mr. Mason could bail me out. I would have gotten in real trouble if I had not seen that woman with the old man in New York."

"… and we were on the way back from Manila when the typhoon caught us. We were in it for three days. There was so much water in the air that you hardly knew where the ocean stopped and the sky started. Every now and then the ship would hang on a wave with the screw out of the water shaking so bad I thought we would fall apart. In the end, everybody was sick below except for me and the old man and we took turns at the wheel. The old man told me, Tom you are best sailor there is."

"… and I was coming home to Tijuana from a card game late one night in a cab with some guys I didn't know. The one in the front seat reached around with a gun and said to give him my money so I picked up a tire iron which was on the floorboard in the back and hit him on the head. I made the driver who might have been in on it drag the man behind some bushes on the side of the road. "

"… and after I got out of the Navy I stayed in Tijuana six months with Rose and Little Tommy and Little Rose. I made a lot of money gambling and from that man and woman who called me over to their big car one day and told me I was a perfect physical specimen and would I get her pregnant because he couldn't do it. (I remembered watching bulls and cows on the farm and figured what the hell.) But after that night in the cab, I had to leave so I gave Rose all the money, 10,000 dollars, and told her I would be back. I went to Shelby for a few months and then to Detroit to work in the Dodge plant. After a year I came back to Tijuana but Rose and the children had left to be with her family deep in the Mexico mountains where I had only been once and couldn't find again."

He sat on the porch, rocking back and forth, drinking coffee that he had brought in the white and blue insulated pot , looking at nothing, smiling a little.

"You did try."

"I got lost. I kept the directions in a shoe box with pictures and other things from down there and somebody stole it on the train to Detroit."

Tom in Mob

Imagining how my father got into and out of the Jack Legs Diamond crime organization...

"God damn son of a bitch."

Tom got behind the wheel of the big black Buick roadster, slid the brown paper bag down from the neck of the Four Roses bottle, twisted off the cap, and took a gulping swallow.

He screwed the cap back on and tucked the bottle under the seat. He didn't want any trouble with the police, not tonight.

There was also the blood on the right sleeve of his white suit. Harry, who worked at Leg's place, where Tom got the bottle after turning in his receipts, had noticed the blood. He had said, "Hey Tommy, ain't it amazing how much a nose will bleed when you hit it hard enough? Maybe them fancy suits ain't such a good idea when you're working."

Tom hadn't said anything, just looked at him, and walked out the door and up the stairs to the alley where he had parked the Buick after coming in from his route.

Leaning forward, he shrugged off the coat. Then folding it so the blood wouldn't show, he laid the garment down on the passenger seat.

Barely keeping up with the cabs, the Buick rumbled softly down Broadway and across to 40 Rector. He parked on the street, not worrying that the car would be bothered by anyone in the neighborhood; people knew who the car belonged to and who he worked for.

The three flights of stairs, which he normally climbed two steps a time, seemed like a mountain tonight. When he got inside the apartment, he didn't turn on the light, just felt his way to the one easy chair and flopped down, clutching the brown bag and the bottle. He wadded up the bag with a quick angry gesture, and threw it across the room, hearing it swat something in the dark. Then he took a long swallow.

Why hadn't the son of a bitch just given him the money? In the six months since Legs Diamond had approached him in the bar about becoming one of his collectors there had been no trouble. He would go to the speakeasy or other place that sold Leg's booze, stare with a hard face at whoever he happened to be talking to, get the payment, and walk out. Simple. It was a good supplement to his regular job as a truck driver for AT&T. His style of living had improved considerably. He wore expensive suits and last month, at Leg's suggestion, he had bought the Buick, paying cash.

Tonight had started out the same as always. The little Italian restaurant in Queens was his third stop, after the two speakeasies. He arrived about seven thirty, when he was sure to catch the proprietor on premises. He double-parked out front, where the Buick could be seen. He didn't expect to be long.

Walking under the street lamp, he noticed that the woman behind the cash register saw him through the front glass. She spoke to somebody out of sight, pointing in his direction.

He pushed open the door, letting it slam behind him.

The woman had been joined by two men, one about her age, maybe mid-forty and the other in his late teens or early twenties. They had an Italian look, almost Indian. Both men wore black suits and had short slick-backed hair cut in the current style. The woman, who, Tom noticed, still had a good figure, wore a tight pale blue dress which went well with her dark hair and skin. She had smiled a little when he first walked in; now she frowned. For a moment he thought about Rose. The older man looked at him with tired, careful eyes. The younger man's mouth was pulled down at the corners and his eyes did not stop blinking. Tom recognized him from previous visits as their son.

The mother and father remained behind the counter; the younger man walked halfway around, his arms folded across his chest.

Tom stared with a hard face at the son until the younger man looked away, pretending to peer at something across the room. Customers, a man and woman with a little boy about six years old approached the cash register, then, ushered by the father, walked quickly back to their table.

Tom turned to the proprietor and his wife and said, "Good evening Mrs. Franco, Mr. Franco. How are yall doin?" He made his voice friendly, drawling out the words. That seemed to confuse people. He didn't ask for the money. They knew why he was here.

The man started to say something, but their son broke in, his words running together, "We're changing suppliers. We're not buying from Legs anymore."

Tom addressed the couple, "That's fine. But you'll have to talk to somebody else about that. I'm just here for your weekly payment. If you'll give me the money I'll be on my way."

The younger man stepped out from the end of the counter and walked forward. He put his right hand into his coat pocket and said, his voice louder, "No. We're not paying you. We'll settle up when we change over." His words seem rehearsed.

Tom shifted his gaze. "No, boy, your folks are paying me, right now. That's the way it is."

The younger man said, "Don't you call me boy, you damn...."

Tom stepped in closer. The mother interrupted, "Alfonz for God's sake....".

"... redneck".

It was if a magic hand passed in front of the younger man's face. The eyes bulged wide, the nose flared, and the mouth started to twist into a grimace. Before the transformation was complete, Tom grabbed the man's wrist, which had just started to move. He felt the tendons tense as the switchblade button was pushed and heard the blade snick open, still inside the coat pocket.

Not letting go of the wrist, which twisted spasmodically in his grip, Tom quickly jabbed the younger man's face. The first punch flattened his nose; the second crunched his right cheekbone. Then, taking his time now, Tom hit him in the stomach, just below the breastbone.

By this time, the mother had run around the counter. While supporting her son with his right hand, Tom used his left hand to lift the now limp wrist from the coat pocket and shake loose the switchblade. Then, after allowing the gasping man to sag to the floor, Tom picked up the knife, closed the blade and placed it with a heavy metallic thunk on the glass top beside the cash register. He said to the father, who stared back with no expression, "Where's the bathroom?"

The man cleared his throat and pointed to the rear, "Back there."

"I'm going to wash off this blood. Have the money ready when I get back."

"God damn son of a bitch."

He lifted the bottle and took another long pull. It wasn't so much that he had to beat up the kid. Hell, he had a knife. Nor had it bothered him in the bathroom, seeing his own hard face in the mirror as he washed off another man's cooling blood. He had done that before.

It had been the little Italian boy sitting with his parents looking wide eyed as he walked by their table. His own son lost somewhere in Mexico would be about that age. After washing off the blood, walking back out through the restaurant Tom had tried to smile at the boy but when the father started to say something, he moved on.

And there was the woman on the floor trying to pat the blood off the ruined face of her foolish son. She reminded him of Rose, the lost mother of his lost boy. This woman hated him, would kill him if she could.

Damn. He took another drink, and put the bottle on the floor beside the chair. He waited for oblivion to settle in. Tomorrow he would forget all this. He would sell the Buick; he didn't care about any of that, and he would tell his boss at AT&T that he wanted a transfer up state.

He would put it out of his mind. He would forget the woman and the man and their son and the little boy and Rose and his own little boy. It would be as if none of it had ever happened.

He went to sleep.

DEATH

1954 – Current

Troy
Shelby

When She Got Sick

Universal collapse...

My mother got sick in August, 1955. She was 44 years old, 24 years younger than I am now.

That something was wrong did not register with me until she had been ill for a week. My universe consisted of other things.

There was the girl, Leanna, who had just gone back to Ohio, and who left behind a permanent association between pine-paneled dens, floral pattern furniture and Prez Prado's song, Cherry Pink and Apple Blossom White. There were the science fiction novels that I had recently discovered. Today the plots of some of those books seem more real than the fuzzy plot of my own life. There was my upcoming Junior year at Troy High School. Part of me had decided not to play football again, but another part knew that if asked, I would probably go out for it – and hopefully this year become a hero in eyes other than my own. There were experiments with shaving, sometimes using my father's double-edge razor and sometimes my uncle's single edge, deciding that although less effective, the single-edge blades were also less painful. There was a summer that sparkled with little transcendent moments.

My parents were shadowy figures at the edges of this universe. As it expanded, they receded, becoming background radiation from my personal Big Bang.

That changed – my old, self-centered universe imploded – the day my mother appeared, in her old house coat, at the entrance to the dining room and announced that she was sick. She had not had a bowel movement in a week and was in pain. I don't remember who was there and who she was talking to. Possibly my father already knew and she was just telling me, or possibly my father, who also lived in his own self-centered universe, had not known and I just happened to overhear her first public announcement of what was ultimately to be her death sentence.

A new, fast-paced universe emerged. Using my memory as an imperfect vehicle for traveling through space and time...

I see the Montgomery County Hospital on a hill up the road from our house. My mother stays overnight while they try to relieve what is first thought to be an intestinal blockage. I can't see the interior of the hospital, just exterior scenes and people – a snowy day when my father tries to drive the old Ford up the hill (sliding back three times before making it over the top), my cousin Betty who lives at the bottom of the hill and who is later crippled in a wreck caused by a drunk driver, a bench on the hospital grounds where I sit with Leanna the last night she is in town.

Next is the Baptist Hospital in Winston Salem. It is a much bigger place. Walking in the front door is like entering a war zone. I know that bad things can happen, but, I am too old to protest.

I see a pale blue hospital room - a bed, a bedside table, my mother smiling. My father is probably there but I don't see him. Because my mother is smiling I assume it is just before her exploratory surgery. Because she would have done that, I imagine she goes out of her way to reassure me, maybe joke about the girl from Ohio. I see her wave when they roll her off, saying that she will see us in a little while.

There is a hospital hallway. My mother is being rolled back into her room. A nurse, wearing a white dress and hat, frowns, as if I am not supposed to witness this. My mother resembles my Uncle Bob the time somebody, maybe my father, beat him up. Her face is red and swollen. A tube of brown urine snakes from under the sheets to a bag hanging on the side of the bed. Other tubes enter her mouth and nose. I say something but she only moans.

I am on my own, roaming the corridors in search of snack bars and exits. I walk by a large room, maybe a conference room. I see the morgue. I leave by a little-used back door, ending up in a nearby neighborhood. It seems like an escape to a magic place. Walking past the neat little houses, watching people doing yard work and attending to ordinary business is like being in another world.

I walk to a restaurant down the street from the hospital. Like the little houses, it also seems to be a pleasant place for happy people, belonging to another world, far removed from here. The restaurant conveys its own emotion, which could be called the "nice little place where I don't belong" feeling. I go inside and order something and think immediately about walking out.

My father, 12-year old sister, and I are in a movie in downtown Winston Salem. My sister is even less aware than me about what is going on and years later, before she too dies, we will talk late into the night about how nobody told her that our mother was deathly ill. I can't concentrate on the movie, only my father's sick smile and my own unease. The drawn dark curtains at the back of the theater remind me of a hearse.

My father and I sit in an office with one or more doctors. It is after the surgery. This place also has its own emotion, possibly the "official place where you get bad news and pretend to be objective" feeling. The doctor explains what they had found. He is kind but officious. My father starts out genial and grandiose then becomes hard and terse. The doctor turns to me. He tells us that it is colon cancer; that they have removed what they can. Nobody says anything about her being dead soon. But that is my understanding.

My father and I go back to Troy. We are in the old Ford. Glancing at me, he tells me I am more mature than my uncle Bob, who lives in the upstairs room across from me and is 14 years older than me. He says that he is depending on me. I mutter something. Although pleased by the praise I am suspicious because I can see no difference between my Uncle Bob and me. I wonder if I am being set up.

When She Died

Bubbles within bubbles...

My new universe expanded. But it was fragile, like a soap bubble. It split every time something bad happened, trapping events within bubbles which were trapped within more bubbles. It was a tainted froth.

One moment we were in Troy. I said goodbye to some people, promising to stay in touch. My father closed my account at the bank. I can see him smiling, letting the prim woman inside the dark oak cage assume that he was me. Forty years later, when he was in a nursing home, covered by a threadbare blanket, I returned the favor, writing checks on his account for the amount not covered by Medicaid, signing our shared name and leaving out the "Junior".

The next moment we were back in Shelby, where family and old friends would help look after my mother. We moved into a little rental house within sight of the hospital.

I think the house was blue. It had two small gable wings pointing toward Lake Street. It was the sort of place that would have appeared in a plan book pored over in the 40's and 50's by members of the Greatest Generation and their war brides. The house looked OK on the outside. However, one wing was never finished. There wasn't a floor, just dirt. My mother and father's bedroom was in the other wing.

My cup bubbled over.

I heard my mother sob, "I don't want to die." I tried not to hear. My father said something. I could feel the vibration of his speech but could not make out his words. The tone was reassuring. Later, when recalling this period, he told an elaborate story about how he and she rode up to the mountains for one last trip and how he told her she was going to die and how she bravely told him that he must carry on. I always wondered how much of it was true.

I saw her changing positions on her bed. I tried not to see. Her gown (I think it was pink flannel) had pulled up. She was not wearing underwear. I could see a red, crescent-shaped scar going all the way across the lower part of her abdomen.

I discovered Angel, the cat, dead on the side of the road. I tried not to care. In our family the animals were people. Angel, a black cat with white around her neck, was a wise old crone. I might have moved her and then told no one so that my mother would not know. But I doubt it. I don't know what happened to Babe, the collie. She probably stayed in the unfinished room. If Angel was a wise woman, Babe was a frightened child who occasionally bit people.

I lay on my bed, consumed by unremitting unease. I had run the family car into a ditch when Doane, Larry and I were out joy riding and my mother had gotten up from her death bed to tell me my father didn't need that. I thought I was going crazy then I threw up and went to sleep.

I tried not to be.

Frothy.

Later in the fall, my mother went into the hospital for the last time and we moved to the old Elk's Club. I don't think she ever entered this house alive. The house, which before it was the Elk's club had been the home of a local lumber baron, was divided down the middle into a duplex. There were large oak trees in the front yard and half the back yard was a gravel parking lot. I suppose it was cheaper than the house on Lake Street although I liked this new place better. The rooms, cut up as they were, still retained some of the original elegance. The entrance to my sister's room was through a set of double doors with glass panes and cut glass knobs. It might have been part of a fancy dining room. My room was just off the big old kitchen. It could have been a butler's pantry. However, that was OK because my desk, bed and chest just fitted and there was an outside door to the back porch.

Probably another reason for moving was because Ma and Teddy Snyder, who once ran a rooming house next door, were kind to my mother and her two younger brothers after their parents died. I expect that my father planned on having her look after my sister and me. I liked Ma Synder and would have liked Teddy if I had been mature enough to appreciate cranky old Yankees. As it was, I thought he was an asshole. This was especially true after my father asked me to climb a ladder to trim one of the trees in the Synder's back yard. I wasn't doing it to suit Teddy and to emphasize his point, he shook the ladder with me standing at the top, holding on to the tree to keep from falling off.

I don't think I visited my mother often after she went in the hospital. My uncle never went. He was afraid. My sister later said that nobody told her what was going on and that she didn't go to the hospital either.

The last time I saw her was two weeks before she died. It was a school night. Ma Synder told me I should go. She went to the hospital every day and my mother might have asked where I had been. I drove myself, parking in the dark lot and finding my way down several corridors to her room. The last corridor was preceded by a low ramp because she was in the new wing where the floor was a few inches higher.

I felt guilty because I had not been to see her more often, and because her face was yellow and purple and my dismay showed, and because I was upright and she was prone and I seemed to be looking down from a great height and she seemed to be absorbed by her bed. I spoke. She threw up black liquid into a kidney-shaped pan. I stepped into the hall while the nurses worked on her. When I got back, one of us might have gotten angry; I don't remember. I don't remember if her voice was still low and throaty, half-educated, half something else. Walking down the hall, I knew I would not be back.

Ma Synder was with my mother the night she died. It was two days before Christmas, 1955. My father had been there, but Ma had told him to go home. She later described, with wonder, how my mother had said "Do you know that doctors bash babies heads against the wall?" then at that moment or perhaps a little later gripped the sheet with her left hand and died.

I was lying on my bed in the former butler's pantry when Teddy and my father woke me. They were backlit by the low winter sun coming in through my window. Teddy, short, broad, with a bushy mustache and Einstein hair, was in front; my father, though bigger, seemed to be hiding.

I don't remember if I got out of bed, or just looked up at them from beneath the covers.

Teddy told me. "Your mother died last night."

Then both of them smiled expectantly, maybe a little embarrassed. Teddy also seemed pleased, as if he had just done a piece of hard work. They waited for me to speak.

I don't know what happened next. Some of the time we were in my room, then in the adjoining kitchen and maybe also on the back porch just outside my room.

It was very frothy, very bubbly.

I could have responded by muttering, "Well, we knew it was coming." And since I am the only one of that trio left alive, it really doesn't matter.

However, it also possible that I threatened to kill one or both of them, which may be the truth since I don't ever remember seeing Teddy after that.

When She Lay Dead

Seeing through lies...

My mother lay dead in a kelly-green dress with sequins on the front. She had worn the dress to a Christmas party at Mr. Daniels' house several years earlier and maybe once again after Shelby Millwork burned and we went to Troy.

The mortician gave her a Mona Lisa smile. In most snapshots she has a puzzled expression.

They put her in the living room, in a cleared area amid a jungle of mums, carnations and baby's breath, lit by a pole lamp on loan from the funeral home.

Maybe she spent the night with us. She had never been in this house. We moved after she went into the hospital for the last time. I seem to remember walking into a room, standing over a coffin, trying to figure out what to feel. I don't remember if the coffin lid was up. It might have been a dream.

Strangers packed the house, full of sympathy and good will. My cousin Buster from Alabama said, "Come on, let's get out of here." We walked out on the porch that wrapped around the front and side of the house. My friend Joe joined us. It was cold and away from everybody else and just beyond the rail, rain came down in a steady gray patter. I wasn't wearing a coat. Buster and I hunched over cigarettes. Buster, who had once been in trouble, grinned and told me something sardonic, maybe about my father.

Christmas morning, the day after the funeral, my father, sister and I gathered in his room in front of the window that looked out on Warren Street. He brought out gifts that he said my mother had made him promise to get. I don't remember my sister's presents. I received a drawing board and a set of German drafting instruments in a black case lined with green velvet. The things immediately acquired the status of sacred family artifacts about which I felt nothing. I used them in a mechanical art class, next year, after we moved to West Palm Beach, and then later, when I drew houses for my father.

A couple of days later, just before everyone left, Uncle Ken asked me to accompany him on a short errand. He was tall and dignified, one of my favorite relatives. During WWII, he had been a Major in the Army and might have made a career in the military if he had not been shot in the foot by a sniper strapped in the top of the same tree against which my uncle reclined (after being killed the Japanese soldier dangled in the fronds like a large dripping fruit).

On our way back, turning the corner onto Lafayette in front of Washington Elementary where we had all gone to school, Uncle Ken mentioned God.

(God is love; God works in mysterious ways; God took her home – something like that.)

I took no comfort from his words and worried that he would see through my lies.

Sunset Cemetery

Where it ends...

Sunset Cemetery is a lovely place. On a clear day from the back part where my mother is buried you can see South Mountain, like a large animal slouching on the horizon.

Once while walking on the Western edge of the cemetery across from where Fluffy the psychiatrist lived before his wife and child left him I saw a raccoon stepping high on its toes to seem taller before disappearing into the brush on the other side of the road.

Another day I heard rumbling thunder when there wasn't a cloud in the sky and walking over the crest of the hill saw a procession of Harley choppers like noisy ghost steeds. The solemn riders leaned back, arms outstretched on ape-hanger handle bars, slowly leaving a memorial for one of their companions.

I taught my daughter to drive in the cemetery, going around and around the winding roads in the old stick shift Volvo, stopping and starting on hills to practice slipping the clutch without rolling back too far.

Ennui Pidawee (being a creature outside of time) still lives on Lee Street across from the cemetery. He takes his uncle's WWII Japanese rifle to the field beyond the Carnation Dairy and dry fires at imaginary soldiers crouched behind head stones on the far hill.

Before my mother died in 1955, the cemetery was a place to play. I observed winos, and rode homemade carts around the twisting curves. In the field where Don Gibson would be buried 55 years later (at the time he was practicing his guitar across the two railroad tracks on the upper end of Lee Street) John Burn wrestled a Daisy BB gun from Buddy Wray then shot him in the ass.

For a long time after my mother's death, I only visited the cemetery when I had to, and then never alone.

In the mid 60's, prompted by my wife, I went with my sister to pick out a stone for our mother's grave. Until then, the only marker had been the card-sized plaque left by the mortuary. After 10 years the card was falling apart. My father paid for the stone but did not get involved in picking it out.

Later in the 60's my sister and I and perhaps her husband and my wife discovered the graves of our mother's parents, BK and Molly, and four of their 11 children (only our mother and three others survived into adulthood). I don't recall what prompted us to make this search. I remember that it was cold in the little outbuilding on the edge of the cemetery where we stood around the sexton's map and found the names BK and Molly. Young and full of purpose we walked briskly up the hill to the Parris plot where the graves were marked by various size rocks (contrasting nicely with the marble mausoleums of the neighboring Schenk family). At the time, none of us made the connection between these unremembered graves and my mother's solitary grave, unnoticed for ten years, or the oddity of mother and daughter both dying young and both managing to leave behind people so anxious to move on, who cared so little (or so much).

In 1980, after being acclimated by Karen Thomas to three-mile lunch-time walks I started taking regular hikes through the cemetery. The first time I was afraid and suffered out-of-body experiences when I confused myself with the dead. Later it was all right.

In 1987, after my heart episode, I crossed Lee Street on the back side of the cemetery and ventured past the three houses where I once lived into the unchanging woods that went unbroken to the river and the bluff where my father once played. Sometimes deep within the tangles and thickets I sensed the possibility of another presence, not knowing then that Pidawee still roamed this bit of wilderness.

Now I visit the cemetery every six months after trips to my dentist, who is in Shelby, and once a year when I take my taxes to the CPA. Out of habit I follow the arc of the dead from BK and Molly, to Curtis and Isabel, to Frank, and then to Eva and Tom.

But I do not think so much about the people I pass. I wonder when and where the circle will close only if my breath going up the long back hill becomes particularly labored.

Otherwise, it is just a walk through a pretty place.